TAKEDOWN

Wendy W. Berry & Jill L. Reiter

Copyright © 2006 by Wendy W. Berry & Jill L. Reiter

All rights reserved. No part of this book shall be reproduced or transmitted in any form or by any means, electronic, mechanical, magnetic, photographic including photocopying, recording or by any information storage and retrieval system, without prior written permission of the publisher. No patent liability is assumed with respect to the use of the information contained herein. Although every precaution has been taken in the preparation of this book, the publisher and author assume no responsibility for errors or omissions. Neither is any liability assumed for damages resulting from the use of the information contained herein.

This is a work of fiction. Names, characters, places, and incidents either are the product of the author's imagination or are used fictitiously. Any resemblance to actual events or locales or persons, living or dead, is entirely coincidental.

ISBN 0-7414-3481-4

Published by:

1094 New DeHaven Street, Suite 100
West Conshohocken, PA 19428-2713
Info@buybooksontheweb.com
www.buybooksontheweb.com
Toll-free (877) BUY BOOK
Local Phone (610) 941-9999
Fax (610) 941-9959

Printed in the United States of America

Printed on Recycled Paper

Published October 2006

BREAKING NEWS: At 7:53 pm Jason Wayne Carter, age 10, was arrested on suspicion of first degree murder in the death of Russell (Rusty) Allen Carter, age nine months. If the information obtained is correct, this will prove to be the youngest child charged with murder in Colorado's history. Reporters are on their way to the scene. Stay tuned for more Nine News updates.

CHAPTER ONE

Jason – Detention

"Hey kid, someone's here to see you."

"Aaaaaaaawwwwwww" I think I'm dreaming, but somebody's making noise. I'm not dreaming. It's the security guard again. Oh man, I'm burning up. I hate this. All I can hear is the sound of bars rattling and big guys yelling to me. Ever since I got to this place, these scums have been yelling, "Hey pretty boy, ain't you a fine one. We never get young blood like you. Bet you've got the virgin one." What are they talking about? At least this cell keeps me safe from them.

"Hey kid, you awake?"

"Yeah. Yeah. Yeah. What are they going to do to me now?"

"Nothing kid. There's a good guy here to see you."

"I don't want to see anybody. I'm finished talking."

"Listen kid, he's on your side."

"Nobody's on my side. Hey, did I miss breakfast? I don't feel so good."

"I don't know anyone who feels great in the morning.

1

Look, I'll get you some grub if you talk to this guy."

"Okay. Who is he?"

"Tom Barrows, your GAL."

This guy looks like he should be playing some music. His brown hair is kinda long and he is dressed in nice jeans. The shirt has a collar, like the ones that Mama has me wear to church, I mean "The Hall." I won't tell him much, but maybe I can get something from him.

"What's a GAL?"

"Hi son. I'm Tom Barrows, you're Guardian Ad Litem. Basically, I'm here to look out for you."

"First of all, don't call me son. And second of all, ain't nobody ever looked out for me."

"Well, in court the judge lots of times assigns a person, usually a lawyer, to help make decisions for you. Man, you got yourself in trouble this time didn't you?"

"I didn't do nothing." "And my lawyer said NOT to talk to nobody."

"Your lawyer actually called me."

"And who's my lawyer, Mr. Bigshot?"

"Well, actually you have two lawyers: Alana Livingston and Michael Kilpatrick."

"So. Okay. You know them. But I'm still not talking to you."

"Okay for today. You need anything?"

"I'm hungry."

"Henry went to get you some food."

"Excuse me Mr. Barrows. Sorry it took me so long. I got him some food and some things for him to clean up with."

"Thanks Henry. Is he sick? He looks shaky and pale."

"No, I don't know. He always wakes up sort out of it and always hot and sweaty."

"Okay. Thanks Henry."

"Look, I said I was hungry."

"Okay. Okay."

CHAPTER TWO

Susan – A Long Night

It was a beautiful spring day that Friday. I was counting the hours until I could head home to the kids. I thought about getting pizza and renting a movie or two. Maybe something light for Megan, a Disney flick, an action movie for me and Joshua to share. Perhaps David would be home and watch with us. Then again, he'd probably spend the night with his best friend Jake. Megan is my only daughter and at the ripe old age of eight is wonderfully wise with the advice she gives me. Joshua is a budding man at fifteen. And David is thirteen, that most difficult age when body and the mind have not yet unified.

I am the clinical director of the Child Psychiatric Unit-Ward 1A at Mount Washington in Denver, Colorado. I always laugh when I introduce myself. It sounds like such an impressive title. Fact of the matter is I'm the head nurse. The only thing that's changed is the year and titles are infinitely more sophisticated. Only the work seems harder and much more intense.

Something was nagging at me. I could leave a little early. After all, the census was twelve. It was quiet. Well staffed. The kids seem to be in a good space. But I found myself busy with catch up paper work. This was, after all, the first time the unit census had been average since January. And then my pager went off. It was the intake office. I was thinking we could use an admission or two. We'd be discharging Ayanna and Marcus on Monday and while budget was rarely my main concern, it was always a close second or third.

"This is Susan. I was paged to this number." I always made sure I was professional on the phone.

"Hi Susan. This is Matt Wilson. I've got a BHS admission for you. This is a six year old boy who tried to jump out of his mother's car after visiting with his bio dad for the first time since his dad got out of jail. Police were called and he became combative with the police. So, get this, they cuffed him and took him to the mental health center. Jay Hamilton evaluated and the child continued to be aggressive and threatened to hang himself if sent home. Jay okayed the admission. He's on his way in."

"Thanks Matt. Sounds like our kind of guy. They cuffed him? Big scary six year old. I'll let staff know. We'll be waiting."

Matt always gave me the pertinent data. For example, BHS is the state subsidized insurance. It stands for Behavioral Health Service. Just enough for me to know what to expect, but not excess information. Theoretically, Matt wasn't obligated to tell me anything except age, insurance, and arrival time. But Matt was a seasoned clinician and he knew the extra information was always helpful. I notified Emily Morgan. Emily was the charge nurse for evening shift. She had worked on the Child Psych Unit for two years. I always felt good leaving the unit when Emily was in charge. Emily had leadership experience in her past. She had gotten completely burned out and decided to get out of management when she moved to Colorado from Kansas. But management was in her blood and she knew how to organize, triage, and get the work done. It was a tremendous comfort to me to have Emily on evenings. Evening could be the quietest of times or the most horrendous. Having a seasoned charge nurse always helped make the difference.

Emily quickly pulled out an admission packet and placed it on top of the desk to be ready. She looked at the bed chart and decided to change some of the children around to make room for this kiddo. She notified Mike Smith, a mental health worker, that two of the kids needed room changes to make space for this one. "Mike, I think we should open up the north end. We can move Ty and Maurice down there. They are both twelve and seem to get along. They are almost ready for discharge and probably don't need as much supervision. This next cherub will bump us to thirteen and we don't have any more space on the south side. What do you think?" Mike quickly agreed and suggested that this would give them one extra room for another admit if necessary. Mike rounded up Ty and Maurice, told them about the room change, and suggested they pack up their belongings for the move. Ty was an African American twelve year old admitted three days ago for hitting his teacher and running away from his foster mother. He too was picked up by the police and brought directly to the unit on a hold. A hold is a seventy-two hour mental health evaluation to assess for mental illness, dangerousness to self or others. The hold was discontinued when the case worker signed him in voluntarily. Maurice, a small blonde with deep brown eyes, was admitted a week earlier for jumping off the balcony of his third story apartment after his father had beaten him with a belt. Surprisingly, he suffered only minor bruising with the fall. His father's wrath left lasting marks. The boys seemed to enjoy each others company and were excited to be moving to a room together. While the rooms were sparsely furnished with beds and dressers, both boys sensed the security on the unit and had settled into the routine well. They both seemed pleased that the staff acknowledged their good behavior and trusted them to be on the side of the unit farthest from the nurse's station.

    My pager went off again. Ah, another typical Friday afternoon. Intake.

    "Hi Susan, Matt again. I've got another one. This one is from Jefferson County. A four year old girl. She was recently placed in her third foster placement in three months. Foster mom noticed that she masturbates constantly and won't eat. This afternoon the girl became very agitated when foster brother took a toy. She started throwing things and couldn't settle down no matter what foster mother did."

"Thanks, Matt. We'll have to do some more creative things with room assignments, but we'll be ready."

I let Emily know about the next admission. Emily smiled and wondered aloud if it was going to be one of those days. "Hmmm. Second admission in less than an hour. What's the record?"

"Six" I said. "Amanda Clark, two weeks ago. I think it was her third night in charge. You know, during the staff meeting last week she said something like that would happen. She must be psychic. Sure enough two nights later she got six admissions during one shift."

Just then my pager went off again. "Here we go," I announced realizing it was intake again.

"Hi Matt. You just called to say hello, right? Long time no see."

"Susan, are you sitting down?"

"Yeah, why?"

"You know that ten year old that's been in the newspaper?"

"Yeah" I replied slowly.

"Well, the court just ordered him to be evaluated here."

"Tell me this is a bad dream."

"I wish I could Susan. I don't know any details, except they are bringing him in under an alias to protect his confidentiality. I don't know anything else yet, but I'll call when I know more."

"Yeah, just call Matt. I'll be here on the unit." I knew this case from the newspaper. I also knew the unit had never done this kind of an evaluation before. I'd better get in gear. It would be a long night. I made a quick list. Call home. Get Joshua to pick up Megan. Suggest he order pizza. That will help him not be so upset that I wouldn't be home as promised. Let Jon know. Jon was the medical director of the unit. He won't be pleased. He hated those cases that the court was involved in. He didn't like spending time testifying. And he didn't like the limelight. Jon was a gentle soul, extremely competent, and a well liked team member. And he was leaving. Four more weeks and he would no longer be the medical director.

Jon was looking forward to spending more time with his family. The job had taken its toll on both he and his family. Being on call, pagers going off at all hours, politics, and sad, sick children had definitely prompted him to reconsider and make changes. And I was incredibly sad to be losing him. I trusted him implicitly. He makes good judgments, is great with kids, and the families like him. I really dreaded calling him about this.

Then there was Leanne. Leanne was my boss. A nurse. Bright, intelligent, seasoned, and opinionated. She'll definitely be upset about this too. Only Leanne will get into action mode to handle her anxiety. That's okay; she'll make sure I don't forget anything. Of course she'll preach and I'll have to make nice, but we'll be covered I thought. I'll also have to notify public relations and security.

The 10 year old Matt was referring to was Jason Wayne Carter. Jason was the youngest child in Colorado ever to be charged with the crime of murder. It happened just two days ago and was splattered all over the newspaper and on the TV. Even his name was released, for reasons that weren't clear to me. Jason's mother had appeared on the news several times adamantly denying that Jason was capable of such a horrendous act. The very sad fact was that a nine month old baby boy was dead. The death occurred in the Carter home. Jason and the little boy were the only ones home at the time of the tragedy. The rest of the information around this case remained a mystery. There was plenty of conjecture about what occurred that night. The media was making it the story of the year. Parents everywhere were holding their babies just a little closer now.

My pager went off again. Matt. "Hi Matt. Do you have more information for us?"

"Yes, Susan. The plan is to bring Mr. Carter in under an alias to protect his identity. The police from the Jefferson Detention Center will bring him here in about an hour and a half assuming all the red tape is cleared up. I'm guessing arrival to be around 1900 hours, maybe later."

"Thanks Matt. We'll be prepared." I took a deep breath and looked at the list and started making calls.

First to Joshua. "Hey Josh. I know you were looking forward to a quiet evening with Mom, but…"

"Oh great. Work again, Mom? You work too much."

"I know sweetie, but this really was not expected and…"

"I know. 'I'll be a little late. Can you pick up Megan?' "

"Well, not exactly. I'm probably going to be a lot late. And can you pick up Megan? She's at Katie's house."

"I know Mom. Right across the street."

"Yup. And Josh?"

"What?"

"Would you like to order pizza?"

"Now you're talking. Pepperoni. Extra cheese. And breadsticks. AND HOT WINGS."

I knew that Joshua would really lay on the guilt and quickly decided some breadsticks and hot wings would help me relieve that guilt a little. Pizza was not a substitute for time and I knew I was going to have to figure out a way to make more hours in the day for the most important people in my life; Josh, David, and Megan.

"Okay Josh. I'm really sorry. I will make it up to you guys."

"I know Mom. You always do. And Mom?"

"Yes Josh."

"David called and he wants to spend the night with Jake. Can he *please*?"

"Yes Josh, he can. I'll call Jake's mom and confirm the plans."

This was actually a good thing. David and Josh were close in age and often competitive. Keeping them separate when I wasn't around was helpful. And Jake's mom, Anne, was a good friend. She completely understood about sibling rivalry; she had four boys of her own.

"Hey, Josh… save some pizza for me. Love you."

"Love you too, Mom."

Okay. The hardest call was out of the way. At least for a moment.

On to Jon. I wondered how I would be able to soften this for him. He really wasn't going to be pleased. I swallowed hard and punched in the number to his pager. Jon responded quickly.

"This is Dr. Hollingsworth. I was paged."

"Hi Jon. Susan. Got a minute?"

"What are you still doing there? I thought you were going to try to get out of there early tonight. It is the weekend after all." Jon had a great telephone voice; soft and melodious, that made you think you could tell him anything. I figured that Jon's voice was one of the reasons he was so good with children. There wasn't an ounce of judgment in his voice.

"Yeah. Best laid plans and all."

"Yes, which is one of the many reasons…"

"I know. One of the many reasons you are out of here."

"Precisely. Well, enough about me. How may I help you Nurse Kiley?"

"Jon we have a tricky situation here. You know the ten year old that's been splattered all over the news?"

"I try not to read the paper, but yes, I think I know the one you're talking about." Jon replied hesitantly.

"Well, the court just ordered him to be evaluated here."

"No Susan. We don't do court ordered evaluations. Send him somewhere else."

"I don't think I can Jon. Matt is trying to figure all that stuff out. Let's assume for a moment that we have to take him."

"Okay. Let's make that assumption. No. I will not take him on as a patient. Don't even think about it. I would suggest that you call Hugh."

"Fine. I'll call Hugh. Anything else I should do?"

"Remind Hugh that we don't do these things. Remind him that these kinds of evaluations are difficult. Get a forensics expert to do the eval. I'd probably segregate him from the other kids, only because of the nature of the crime and to protect his confidentiality. Anyone admitted after Wednesday is going to recognize him in a heartbeat. And Susan?"

"Yes, Jon?"

"Try to take care of yourself through this. I'm sorry you're going to have to go through this. It's a messy business at best, but this is really tough."

"Thanks, Jon. Do you want to be kept up to date on

this?"

"Just the necessary stuff. I'll be available to you, but try not to have the others involve me. Okay?"

"Okay. I'll leave voice mails through the evening hours and weekend. That way I won't wake the whole household with pages at all hours. Will that work?"

"Thanks, Susan. I'll check the messages often."

I knew that Jon's hands were full with an ill wife and three growing children of his own. Elaine Hollingsworth had been diagnosed with lupus last year and the entire family was attempting to adjust to life with a chronic illness. Elaine had been the rock of the family and now was having to allow Jon to step in and offer help more often. This was one of the bigger factors in Jon's recent resignation. There were others.

"Okay, Jon. I'm going to work on the rest of this list. I'll talk with you later."

"Okay. Take care Susan."

"Thanks, Jon. Bye now."

Okay. Leanne. Take a breath, Susan, and call Leanne. I paged her, public relations, and security. Then I sat back and waited for return calls. First Leanne.

"Hello. This is Leanne Bartholomew. I was paged."

"Hi Leanne."

"Oh, hi Susan. What's up on this gorgeous Friday afternoon?"

"Thanks for calling so quickly. I needed to let you know we are in the process of getting a tough case."

"What's new?" she quipped.

"I know. But this could be high profile. You know the ten year old in the paper yesterday?"

"Oh. I get it. What a nightmare. You don't want

this case. I'm telling you, the staff will react. You'll have to pay attention, Susan. Really, this is a nightmare. Can we say no?"

"I don't think so. Matt Wilson is getting details, but it's a court order. I wasn't under the impression that we could say no to the court."

"Well, you may be right. I know Hugh asked this question before. We'll have to check that out with the hospital lawyer. You'll need to call security and don't forget PR."

"I've got pages into both. Hugh is on call and I'm getting ready to notify him next."

"Good. Well, good luck. If there's any way not to take this case, do it. The staff will react. I've done this before. It's not pretty."

"Thanks, Leanne. I'll call you when I've got more details."

The next two phone calls were standard. Security took the information and so did Kay Morris from Public Relations. Kay advised me to call her if I became aware of any leaks. She also promised to call if the media got a hold of the story.

My next page went to Hugh. Hugh O'Neil was the Chairman of the Department. He was in his mid forties and had moved to Colorado from Maine three years ago. Hugh and his wife had their first child six months earlier. He was a proud father and enjoyed showing pictures of his son to staff. This was somewhat uncharacteristic of him, since he was ordinarily a private person. Fatherhood seemed to help him relax some and become more human in the eyes of the staff. Hugh's response to the news was grounding. He confirmed my thought that indeed the hospital was not in a position to say no to the court. He also spent a fair amount of time talking with me about maintaining the boy's confidentiality and also maintaining a safe environment for the remainder of the milieu.

Milieu is a term used in psych to describe the environment. Books have been written about the subject, but to me the concept was a simple one. Were the children feeling safe or not? Generally, if kids were feeling safe the milieu was relatively orderly. If, on the other hand, the kids were not feeling safe a variety of things could happen: patients could act out, become violent, become needy and whiny, demonstrate regressive behaviors, just to name a few. Staff spent a lot of time paying attention to milieu and the impact that each patient and staff had on milieu.

Hugh and I decided that the boy would need to be isolated from the remainder of the group, in order to pay attention to milieu and confidentiality. We also knew that we had never had a case like this on the unit and we didn't know exactly what to expect.

The pager went off again. Matt.

"Hi Matt."

"Hi Susan. Our boy is on his way. He'll be admitted under the name of Timothy Basil. I'll notify admissions."

"Okay. I'll let security know. By the way, who's guaranteeing this admission?"

"Good question, Susan. Let me find out. They faxed the Court Order over and I'll get that to you."

"Thanks Matt. Hey, Matt thanks for doing such a good job on this."

"Sure, Susan. Just doing my job."

I decided I'd better pull the staff together and let them know about Timothy. Emily had just finished up with the other two admissions and was having one of the mental health counselors orient the new kids to the program. It was important for new patients to understand that staff was there to keep everyone safe, that everyone should be respectful, as well as the nuts and bolts of where things were, and when meetings, meals, and quiet time were happening. When Emily walked by into the nurse's station she noticed my expression.

"Yo. Susan. It's six thirty, what are you still doing here?"

"Well, funny you ask. Can you get the four of you together for a quick update?"

"Sure, but this doesn't sound good."

"Well, it's not bad, it just needs attention."

Brady—also a nurse, Emily, mental health counselors Debbie and Mike, all walked into the nurse's station looking grim. I shared the news: admission number three was on his way. I also shared what little I knew about the case. After the initial dismay, there was a flurry of questions.

"What about the other kids?" Mike questioned.

"What about the parents?" chimed in Debbie.

"How are we going to maintain confidentiality?" Emily added.

"Staffing?" Mike asked.

I quietly went over the plans. Timothy would be separated from the rest of the patients. This would help to ensure his safety and confidentiality. It would also help us to maintain the safety of the other patients. Maintaining confidentiality would be tough. His chart would be locked in a cabinet, only regular staff would interact with him, and he would be assigned one staff at all times. This was called a one-to-one. One-to-ones were usually ordered when there was a concern about suicide or self-harming. It was the best way to maintain safety when the stakes were high.

I ordered pizza for the staff and settled into writing a plan for Mr. Basil's admission. Staff used their anxiety to make sure kids were safe, rooms were assigned, and the unit was functioning effectively. The kids on the unit, with the exception of the two new admits, were stable and relatively cooperative. These children, like so many of the children that passed through these doors, often calmed quickly in the presence of structure and safety. Generally, the children admitted to Ward 1A were in crisis; either victims of family chaos or contributors to it. And like the cycle of abuse in all forms, victims frequently become perpetrators in order to feel some control, keeping the cycle just that – a cycle. But crisis, no matter what the cause, is self limiting. And providing consistency and predictability helps the child in crisis overcome and regain control.

The new admits looked exhausted and would likely settle quickly into the routine. I praised the staff for their good work and calm demeanor even though internally they were anything but calm. Pizza arrived and was gratefully consumed. Staff anticipated the need for nourishment knowing the night was likely to be long.

Matt Wilson called back and said that the court decided to wait until tomorrow to admit young Mr. Basil in hopes to keep the media out of the way.

I let staff know about the delay. They all sighed in relief, but knew that it was only a momentary stay.

CHAPTER THREE

Adrianna – Dragon's Eyes

2:33 a.m.: The glaring red numbers on my clock look like dragon's eyes. These long nights with fitful sleep were wearing on me. I hardly remember a night that did not contain nightmares and sheets wet with sweat. As I lay awake, body aching from tossing and turning, I remember a time that was much simpler. The days of planning therapeutic activities for troubled young souls. We were a good team in Psych Ward 1A. We worked collectively to teach these children to express themselves with words, rather than the behavior that so plagued their existence. Some severely damaged by abuse, others spoiled teenagers unable to get their way. The professionals at Ward 1A were cohesive, bright, and worked on the cutting edge to effectively change the lives of families. That was the better part of the memory.

The sunrise was spectacular, though no time to enjoy it. I had obviously drifted back into somewhat of a restful state. I was due at the courthouse once again for an 8:00 a.m. pretrial. The courts had such a backlog of cases, we were being asked to do preliminary work on Saturdays. Rushing through my morning shower, my dog Grouchow was guarding the door. He was a 180 lb English Mastiff. The most docile and loving dog I had ever come in contact with, but looked like he could eat a grown man in three bites. Coffee in the "to go cup" and out the door. Thank someone for inventing those wonderful automatic coffee makers with a timer. The kids and Carl still asleep, I escape without interaction with the family.

Cell phone in hand I begin to retrieve messages from the night before. Many of them mundane and able to be put off. My third message however, made my hair stand on end.

It was a voice from what I had hoped always to be the past. Brady Phillips was a Psychiatric RN that I had worked with years before. We were a team on the 3-11 shift early in my career. Brady and I frequently went for a drink after work to wind down and process our night. There were others, and all of us good friends. I knew immediately that there was something amiss. Brady had that serene calm voice until something was wrong. Then he was coarse and abrupt and all business. This time, Brady sounded different, shaken. He was not going to leave details on an unsecured line, but needed me to call him ASAP.

Traffic was horrendous. Terminal construction, in a city that had no business growing any larger at this time. Denver, once a cow town, now a metropolis, was booming. It was on these days that I missed my roots. The beautiful green 100 year old trees and farmland of Ohio. Drifting into daydream, I was interrupted by a loud honking from my right. Sorry! I was so tired of saying that word. Realizing that I was stretched beyond my limits right now and not giving my all to anything.

Running a household was a full time job with three boys, all very active. Jonah now 16 could help with the driving, but Jacob and Jackson my 10-year-old twins, were too distracting to allow Jonah to drive them anywhere. They all play hockey, almost every day of the year. The twins now on separate teams, with one playing AA travel hockey. Add homework and day-to-day activities, I am spent by 8 p.m.

Now working solely in private practice I have stress beyond what the charts say is tolerable. We moved to the suburbs shortly after that unforgettable day. Carl thought that this would help me feel safe and secure. The kids were frightened and we all agreed, reluctantly, that a change was necessary for us all to move forward and let go of the heinous memories. I commuted to the city with thoughts of continuing my professional private practice there. The commute was really hard on me and the kids. Carl of course was not there. I finally gave in and found office space in our little community. Fortunately the town grew very quickly and my services were in high demand. I began to switch from child and adolescent therapy to child custody evaluations and high conflict divorce. I was one of the few in a fairly large county to have the experience, and with difficult cases. The judges began to refer all of the families with extreme therapeutic needs to me. Somehow my practice grew from part time to full time in three months. Yes, I was overextended in every area of my life.

    I attempted to reach Brady several times on my way to the courthouse. I only got his voice mail. Trying to come up with something casual to say, I hung up without words each time I heard the recording. I still ached at the thought of our last encounter. I secretly fantasized about a rendezvous regardless of the obvious consequences. Brady would always make me wonder what could have been. Our relationship was incredibly passionate, but obsessive and ultimately unhealthy. He was now married to a woman so jealous of my existence that our only contact had to remain secretive. This added a touch of mystery and adventure to our sporadic flirtatious interactions.

    Once again, daydreaming. My car on autopilot, I head into heavier traffic. My thoughts drift to daily life almost three years ago. Life was simpler and I had time with the kids. My husband and I had been drifting apart for sometime. He is a Wall Street Broker and traveled four out of seven days. I was lonely and Brady was there. We were great friends until we realized that we were in love. The passion was something that I had been missing for years. I had to reach Brady soon. There was something urgent in his voice.

    The courthouse was quiet and parking a breeze. This was not the norm; no metal detectors blaring, just the security guard meeting us at the south entrance. Today these walls would have a bit of respite.

I would be testifying as an expert on child custody in a highly contentious divorce. These people had spent over $600,000 fighting with each other and screwing up their kids in the process. Once again my testimony would be hailed by one and detested by the other. Judge Days was one of the oldest and most inappropriate left in the system. She was known for her power plays and for her relentless lectures, most of which were off base. My work was well regarded by her, but this was no assurance that I would not become the object of her wrath. Hopefully this would be whittled down today, so that my testimony on Monday would be brief.

Eleven AM and the meeting finally concludes. What a production these people make out of the most miniscule issue. I should have figured, with the attorneys involved, that it would be a real pissing match. The lawyer that I despised made every one of his women clients a victim of severe domestic violence. He, of course, would rescue them and then explain to the court that he would never allow children to have contact with the evil ogre that they knew as their father. The games and politics in the courtroom continued to amaze me. The attorneys would battle it out, using sarcasm, low blows and even lies. Glaring at one another, in the eyes of the court they were outright enemies. Leaving the courtroom seemed to have some amazing magic that would render these lawyers with amnesia because they instantly became old pals. How could this really be justice with more drama than truth?

The good news was that I was out of there for the day. I will head to the office with only paper work and phone calls to return. I turned my cell phone back on, actually happy to see that there was a message. Hopefully Brady. Pushing in my code without even thinking, I began to feel that old body sensation. The excitement and anticipation of hearing his voice. Yes it was Brady, but again very short with no warmth in his voice. We had gone through so much together that there were often times that he was cold and defensive. We tried to pretend that our relationship was without expectations, only to find that this was impossible.

Dialing his number I felt the urge to ask him to meet me. His voice sounded so serious.

"Hello, Brady here".

I was startled to hear him answer. "Brady, hi, it's me Adrianna."

"Oh Adrianna, I am sure that you have been reading the news. It's not something that I can really talk about, but wanted to forewarn you that you may be asked to consult."

"What are you talking about; I have no idea what is in the news. Come to think of it, the kids, Carl and I took off Thursday for an overnight in Vail. I have not seen a thing. What is it Brady?"

"Well, first of all, thanks for the details of the old happy family. The headlines are still dripping with ooze about a case. A very interesting case. Maybe you should grab a paper Adrianna."

"Cut the sarcasm Brady, you called me, remember?"

"Sorry Adrianna, you threw me with the vision of you and well, you know. Just get a copy of the last few days' papers."

"I appreciate the tip, but you sound so intense, consults don't usually stop my life in its tracks."

"Sure. Whatever. This one may be different, trust me."

"Thanks Brady, maybe we will run into each other, if I receive any requests from the Mount for a special consult."

"It's been awhile Addy, I would like to work together on a case again, and I think that we could keep it professional now."

"Sorry to hear that Brade, I was hoping to have hot passionate sex in the day room or the janitorial closet after a staffing."

"Goodbye Adrianna."

"Goodbye Brady."

Why did I always have to test to see if it was still there with him? I knew it was and he knew it was, and it just caused more pain for both of us. At least he called me Addy again. That was his softer side. If only he would not have married her. Who am I kidding? That is what saved my marriage and kept me out of the ugly divorce court that I work in daily. Thank God I don't have to fight for my kids. Now, what is Brady referring to? I better get a News.

Starbucks was on the way to my office and what better place to get a treat along with my paper. No wait to order.

"I will have a grande, nonfat, peppermint latte please."

I went to get the paper, as my beverage was brewing and almost gasped at the headlines.

"YOUNGEST CHILD MURDERER IN COLORADO HISTORY- BRING IN THE SPECIALISTS" The subtitles were haunting.

"Excuse me Ma'am? Your latte is ready."

Again I was lost in my own world. "Thank you, I also need a News". I left quickly. Was this what Brady was alluding to? There is no way that Mt. Washington would accept an admission with this high profile. There are criminal psychologists to deal with this in the detention centers. No way would I ever accept a consult like this, but I do really enjoy going back to the Mount on occasion.

Susan Kiley and I had become great friends. She was

the Clinical Director of the Child Psychiatric Unit at Mount Washington. We connected instantly, even during my initial interview. Our friendship developed quickly and we still get together when time allows. Susan had a very secret and dark home life; one that she shared with very few people. She was able to compartmentalize her life and never showed signs of the stress that she was under. Her work was exemplary. She was extremely thorough in her assessments and almost always right on. We were a great team, balancing each other out with our different perspectives. She was one person I knew I could trust with my professional opinions, even when they were built on intuition alone.

Once again lost in thoughts of the past. I really need to stay focused. I have so much report writing to get to and so little time as it is. Daydreaming is for those who have the luxury of time. Finally at my office, I begin to unload the day's files. This is the space where I seem to find the most comfort. How crazy is that? The place where I hear about, and experience first hand, the chaos and turmoil that the majority of our population is in. I have furnished my second floor, corner office with antique cherry furniture and oversized chairs. My lamps don handmade lampshades from the orient and seem to send off their own feeling of comfort and warmth. The subtle shade of moss green on the walls reminds me of the grounding force of nature. I have bookshelves lined with everything from Anatomy to my favorite children's book: *Brave Bart*.

Breathing a heavy sigh, I close my door so as not to be disturbed. I light my candles and put my files away. My gaze moves to the 3x5 black and white photos in the center cubby of my desk. My boys at the beach. I stare at their happy dancing eyes, lit up with love and innocence. Every year we spend time at the beach house in the Outer Banks of North Carolina. The beaches are undisturbed and usually set the stage for a very relaxing few weeks. Our boys are content to boogie board and build sandcastles. Regardless of their age difference and the fact that they are now much older, this is one place that seems to bring us together as a family. Oh how I wish that we were all there now.

I will really put some parameters on my time here today. I move into a daydream and begin to relive last night. My phone had rung and it was the boys.

"Hi Mom, you said that you would be home for dinner, its 7:30 pm." The sound of disappointment in Jackson's voice was evident.

"You missed the parent meeting at our school about the 5th grade week at camp." "I'm sorry honey, I was in……"

"I know Mom, in court again."

"I'm truly sorry Jackson, I will pack up and be home in 10 minutes."

"Honey, its me, we talked about this late night at the office thing, it's really not good for any of us."

"Hi Carl, I know, I am on my way, I just had some things to catch up on." Silence. A click.

I had blown out the candles, turned out the lights and had not even wanted to go home. The object of everyone's disappointment once again and still facing hours of unfinished paperwork. Knowing that they had already eaten, I punished myself further with fast food. The drive-through had become my friend. I decided to try to sooth my mind with music. I turned on the radio, only to hear Love Shack by the B 52's. Oh yeah, that's what I am going home to I had thought, a regular Love Shack. Knowing that sarcasm is my defense I realized that a quick change of attitude, focused on an apologetic theme was necessary. As I unwrapped my burger a thought hit me; I would arrange for a long weekend at the beach house and my spontaneous gesture will make up for my lack of availability lately. I remember pulling into the driveway, long and tree lined, thinking of my grandfather's farm. As I had neared the house I saw that there was an unfamiliar car in the driveway. Maybe a friend of Jonah's working on a school project. The kids all go to private school and Jonah is in all honors courses. He is very bright and has his sights set on Duke or Stanford. If anyone can do it he can. He is disciplined, almost to an extreme. Hockey is the one thing that he seems to do outside of academics, yet is still hard on himself as a varsity-starting center. Pulling into the garage I had a sinking feeling and the burger seemed to revisit its route through my esophagus.

I entered through the laundry/mud room. The kitchen was dark and closed for the night. I noticed that the lights in the back patio area were on and there was laughing. I heard a female voice that I did not recognize. Quietly I made my way through the family room where the fireplace was lit and snacks lay on the table. Nobody was inside, not even Grouchow. How strange. I made my way to the French doors that lead to the back patio and pool area. I saw my family and a beautiful blonde young lady. Grouchow noticed me and slowly made his way to say hello. He was drooling which meant that someone had been treating him to table scraps.

"Hello" I managed to say quietly. Jonah jumped up and forced a smile.

"Hi Mom, I would like you to meet my friend, Ashley."

Trying to pull myself together and realizing that I missed more than the 5th grade camp meeting, I mustered the energy to give Ashley the required warm welcome. This was very uncomfortable. I felt like an outsider in my own home. Had I missed the planning of the debut of Jonah's first girlfriend? Or was the family so tired of my absence that they chose not to include me in major family events anymore? I had to admit she was stunning. She was not the meek little mousy type that so many girls her age tried to be. She carried herself with confidence. I liked that.

Carl had not made eye contact, Jackson and Jacob finally came over to give me a hug. I whispered quietly "I love you and I am sorry about tonight." They are still very forgiving and both gave me an "its okay Mom look". Jonah had waited for a moment and politely asked if I would like to join them. He explained that Ashley had made the state finals for tennis. She would be playing next weekend in Beaver Creek and wondered if we would like to go. I was caught totally off guard, remembering my plan to whisk the family off to Duck, North Carolina. I guess I really have been missing the boat. My kids are moving on with their lives and cannot possibly go away without proper notice; their social lives would certainly suffer.

I had felt obligated to participate in this family interaction, yet longed to retreat to a bubble bath and good book. Carl finally moved in my direction, offering to get me a glass of wine. The twins were busy trying to tell me about their new coaches, and Brady still weighed heavy on my mind. Ashley was talking to Jonah about her potential competition. I watched him, amazed at his maturity. He was reassuring and genuine. He seemed to have an almost hypnotic effect on her. WOW, I had never seen this side of him.

I remember sitting, rather chilled in the night air. Ashley and Jonah were sitting closer now. For the very first time, I saw him as an individual, as a young man. He would be on his own soon making choices for himself without the parental units watching over him. It was time to give him the space to grow.

Now the dilemma of the long weekend. Do we all go to support Ashley? This is ultimately supporting Jonah. Or do we, Carl and I, take the twins in an attempt to solidify our family unit? I had thought that sleeping on this information would help me sort it out.

I told myself to stop the review of the past twenty-four hours right there, but rumination was a common problem with me. This morning I got into my car and realized that I had set aside the *News* and had not yet even begun to investigate what Brady was talking about. My phone had begun to ring again and interrupted the organization of my day.

"Hello, this is Adrianna."

"Addy its Carl, we really need to talk about things."

"Oh here we go, Carl, look, I apologized for being late, I was swamped and…"

"No, Addy, its not just me that you are affecting with all of this, the kids are suffering."

Blowing out all of the air in my body, I bit my tongue and tried to be positive. "I know that I have been busy Carl. I have put out the word that I am not taking any really difficult cases for awhile. That should free me up a bit."

"Addy, it's not just that you are busy, you are distracted, emotionally unavailable. I have gotten used to it, but the kids need you."

"Well, I was going to surprise you all with tickets to the beach this weekend, but I am torn between that and Jonah's girlfriend's tennis tournament.

"Geography is not going to cure what you have done to this family Addy."

"Oh, hey Carl, can you hang on? I am getting another call."

"No Adrianna, this is exactly what I am talking about, get your priorities straight."

Click. The other line had continued to ring; I had no energy to answer.

The sun had been beaming through my sunglasses. My head was throbbing; I had tried to gather my thoughts. I set my latte in the drink holder, and started the car. Cool air and some Crosby Stills and Nash should put me back on track. Please tell me that noise is not my phone ringing again. Damn that Carl, he does this every time.

"What?" I answered.

"Whoa, whoa, whoa Missy, that's no way to say hello to an old friend!"

"Susan?"

"Yeah, honey that be me."

We have always had these funny accents that we use with each other. Her horrible sounding southern, British flare made me laugh.

"I am so glad you called, your timing is impeccable."

"Oh let me guess, this time on a Saturday morning it could only be Carl?"

"Of course, but let's not go there, and please tell me that you are calling about a girl's night out."

"Well, not exactly. We need your expertise back on the unit."

"Oh Susan, sorry, but that is part of the problem. My home life is suffering and the kids are even mad now."

"Look Missy, I can't take no for an answer on this one. Hugh and Jon both agree, it has to be you."

"You have got to be kidding, is this the…" Susan quickly interrupts me.

"Ssshhhh … we need to talk in person. ASAP."

I had tried to explain to her that number one it was Saturday, and that number two I was already in the dog house with my family. She would have nothing of it and more or less demanded that I meet her in her office by 2:00 p.m.

CHAPTER FOUR

Jason -Hospitalization

"Hey kid. Get up. Get ready to go."

"Whaaat? What are you talking about? Where am I going?"

"You'll find out. Just get up and get ready."

I try to do what they tell me. I mean I figure its better that way. Just do as I'm told. That's why me and mom do okay. I just do what I'm told.

I see that guy again. The GAL dude.

"Where am I going, Mr. ummm. I guess I forgot your name."

"Mr. Barrows, son. The guards are going to take you to Mount Washington. Have you heard of Mount Washington?"

"Yeah. It's where crazy people go. I ain't no crazy."

"Well, that's not exactly right. It's where people go who have problems. The people there can help kids and parents who have problems."

"Well, I ain't got no problems and neither does my mom, asshole."

"Watch your mouth youngster. I need you to listen to me now, okay?"

"I am listening, okay?"

"The people at Mount Washington are there to help you. They are also there to help the court figure out what's best for you. The thing you have to remember is that you are NOT to talk to ANYONE about what happened. Got that?"

"Yeah. So, what am I supposed to talk about?"

"Well, they will probably ask you lots of questions about friends, school, your family, things like that. You should be honest about all of that. You can tell them what you're charged with, but nothing about what happened."

"What am I charged with? I heard the judge and lawyers talking, but I don't remember exactly what they said."

"That's understandable, son. You are charged with first degree murder."

"Oh." I didn't want for him to think that I was stupid, so I didn't ask him what the first degree was for. I guess that just means its real bad.

"So, when am I going to that place?"

"In just a few minutes."

The guards came in just then and put this bar things on my legs. It made it real hard to walk. They cuffed me again like when they picked me up at my home. I just wanted to be back home. I'm tired of feeling scared all the time. I just want to go home. In a few minutes I'm in this van and we're driving. It's almost morning time. It's the time I used to like the best. Almost finished with a night and daylight is coming. But I don't know when I'm going to finish this day. Or the next.

We get to Mount Washington and they take me to this place called Ward 1A. Some lady there looks like she's about to cry when she sees me. She tells the guard to take this jail stuff off my arms and legs before I come in the unit. She asks me my name. I tell her, "Timothy Basil". Then I tell her, "It's not my real name you know." She says she knows, but says it's good that I remembered to use the name they told me to. She walks me down this real long hallway to a room. It's a nice room. It's got a bed and a place to put your clothes and stuff, 'cept I don't have no clothes. Just this stupid orange thing that's too big. She gives me some clothes to put on so I don't have to wear this stupid orange thing. She goes away so I can change.

When she comes back she takes the orange thing and puts it in a bag. I don't act like I like it here, but it sure is different. It's for sure better than jail and well, it's cleaner than home.

She asks me if I'm hungry. I tell her yes. I get some graham crackers and milk. She gets this guy named Mike and tells me that he's going to stay with me for the rest of the day. She says he'll stay outside my door while I sleep. I don't say anything. I think maybe I can sleep tonight.

CHAPTER FIVE

Susan - Reflections

I left the unit at 9:30p.m. Hopefully Josh would still be up so I could talk with him a little while. The ride home was quiet and peaceful. I took side streets all the way home so as to avoid the night construction crews of T-Rex on the freeways. Denver's spring evenings were almost as lovely as the days—cooler temperatures, no humidity. I opened the windows of my Honda and enjoyed the breeze all the way home.

Sure enough, Josh was watching sports when I arrived home. Megan had fallen asleep on the couch and had Snow and Flake, our two Bichon Friese puppies, snuggled on either side of her. Josh was on the other couch and was munching from a big bowl of freshly popped popcorn sitting on the end table.

"Hi Mom."

"Hi Josh. Thanks for being my favorite oldest son in the whole world."

"Oh Mom, thanks for being my favorite mom in the whole world."

"Welcome to the world's favorite admiration club."

"Yep."

"So, how was your day?"

"Fine."

"That good?"

"Yup. It's always best on Saturdays."

"Same with me. I thought I'd be home early."

"Riiiggghhhhhttt. I've heard that one before."

"I know. But I really did think… Oh well. I won't go there. Are there any good pay per view movies you want to watch tonight?"

"Would that be with you or without you?"

"What's your pleasure?"

"With you."

"Sounds good to me. Let me change my clothes and I'll be right back. You pick. Just make sure it's…"

"I know, Mom… APPROPRIATE."

"Yup. That's the ticket."

He chose *Fast and Furious*.

As we watched, I found myself distracted and pondering the day. Wondering how the next few days would go with our new patient, wondering if the media would find out where this youngster was and if I'd be on the phone with public relations. I knew one thing – I had to get Adrianna to consult on this case. Since Jon refused to take the case it meant Hugh would most likely take the case. I was worried. Hugh had a new baby. I could imagine how that might affect his thought processes. Oh, he'd say he'd be objective, goodness knows we all want to be, but what would it be like for him to interview a child accused of killing a baby? Adrianna Jones could add objectivity to this case. Her diagnostic skills were impeccable. She'd consulted on high profile cases in the past and done well, both with the case and the media. I'd have to do a sales job to get her to do it, but I knew she would. After all, she and I had a history few friends had.

I was haunted by the thought of this youngster killing a baby. I reflected on my own children. I tried to imagine that horror. I couldn't. My family had been through its own hell, but nothing like this. I could only imagine what it was like for this child to be in jail, with no peers. What were his parents feeling? Where were they? I knew that in time I'd know the answers to these questions; I wasn't sure I was prepared to hear them.

    I was tired, but the adrenalin effects lived on. I tried to anticipate the extra staffing that would be needed; the additional security on the unit, making sure this child was guaranteed privacy. I worried that if families were aware who this patient was, they'd fear leaving their child on the unit. Having a child hospitalized psychiatrically is a very difficult thing. Parents frequently feel guilty that they've done something wrong; that they've somehow made their child get to this point. Sometimes parents have contributed to the problems, often it's a combination of genetics and the environment. Finding out that a "baby killer" was on the unit, would make them infinitely more concerned. I hoped that this admission would go smoothly, that we could maintain this child's confidentiality that the media would not find out where he was. It was hard to imagine that this would go well.

    Joshua seemed to be dosing off while watching the movie. I asked him if he wanted to finish it. He said, "No. I've already seen it three times; I just wanted you to see it." I told him I'd finish the ending in the morning. He seemed satisfied with that. I carried Megan to bed. Snow and Flake followed and quickly resettled next to her upstairs in her room. I kissed her forehead and realized once again how blessed I was to have her. I then went to Josh's room and stood at the door as he got into bed. I told him I loved him. He replied, "ditto", and I turned out his light and went to my room.

CHAPTER SIX

Adrianna – The Meeting

My car was warm from the spring sun. The drive shouldn't be brutal this time of day but in Denver it is always hard to predict. There could be a Rockies game, it is Saturday. I decide to turn the radio off and go over my strategy and refusal with Susan. There is no way that I can take this case. Carl and the kids have been pushed to their limit. I am going armed with the latest pictures of the kids. This will certainly make an impact. Susan will understand; she has had her share of family turmoil.

The entry to Ward 1A is marked only by a buzzer and intercom system.

"Hello, may I help you?" the very pleasant and comforting voice of Doris. She is a 60 year old African American female who keeps the unit running smoothly as the Ward Clerk. Doris is now raising her three grandchildren and taking care of her husband who had a stroke only six months ago. She is one of the strongest and most positive women I have ever met.

"Hi Doris, I am here to see Susan."

"Well if it isn't the lone ranger. How you doin girl?"

"How 'bout you let me in and we can chat about life in the burbs." Doris knew how I felt about leaving the city. I have never been keen on those cookie cutter neighborhoods and covenant controls. I would complain to her that there was no culture, no diversity out there. Doris, with her great sense of humor would tell me that I was diverse enough for a whole community and that I would be "spicing up the town".

Entering the unit, I notice that the south end of the unit has brown paper covering the windows. Probably more construction. This end of the unit has been ready for a face lift for some time now. The patients were eating in the day room and the unit seemed full. Doris met me in the hall with a welcome hug.

"Now girl, I know you brought pictures of those babies of yours."

"Oh Doris, babies no more, Jonah is driving and has a girlfriend. The twins look like line backers; the hockey clubs have started a weight program."

"Oh my! How is Carl?" She asks tentatively.

"Great, just fine, terrific in fact."

"Things are that bad huh?"

Just then Susan interrupts, "Okay ladies, sorry to break up the coffee clutch, but Addy and I have some work to take care of."

"Well hello to you too and great to see you again. Uh oh, I guess I better go Doris, we will catch up later."

Susan escorted me to her office. Walking through the unit, we tried to maintain a professional demeanor. Once inside her office, Susan and I gave each other a quick hug.

"I feel like I'm always dragging you into something dark," she said.

"Then don't."

"Wow, I wasn't expecting that. What's going on?"

"Look, bottom line is Carl wants me to quit altogether. This could be the last straw. Things are very tense at home."

"Understandable. But this child's life could literally depend on the assessment that's done here. You know Jon's not going to take this case. Hugh's doing it."

"Oh, I get it. But Susan, I know nothing about this. I've barely read the headlines. We were in Vail when it happened. I'd be starting from scratch."

36

"Better yet, you won't be contaminated."

"Damn it Susan, you have a response for everything! How long?"

"A week. Tops. A court order requires the reports be in by Wednesday. You can start now and work through the weekend. With the press the way it is, we have our best shot at keeping this under wraps and quickly getting as much as we can."

"What about court?"

"Taken care of. We won't even have to testify. Hugh and Gene will be considered the experts. We'll just be behind the scenes. Melissa Rubenstein has already been consulted. She says and I quote: 'this is the boy's case, are we clear?'"

"Get out"

"No. That's exactly what she said. But it makes it all the easier for you. And me too. Lord knows I don't need anyone from the media bothering me."

Just then there was a knock at the door.

"Uh, sorry to interrupt Susan, but I just did the count. It's off again,"

Susan looked up at Brady and it was clear he wasn't expecting me to be sitting there. Our eyes met and then he quickly looked back at Susan. She probably felt like an unwanted visitor. Susan knew of my affair with Brady. Fortunately Brady was unaware that she knew. Susan cleared her throat, obviously stressed.

"Ritalin again?"

"Of course", Brady mumbled unable to take his eyes off of me. "I counted it last night and it was fine."

"Well, write up an incident report. Please keep this quiet. We'll need to figure this out later."

Brady exited without another word.

As the door closed I was staring out the window, lost in thought, lingering in moments of the past. I decided not to go there. Susan was talking, "Hello space case, anyone in there? Still a distraction is he?"

"Of course not, why would fond romantic memories be a distraction?"

"So. Let me fill you in on what I know."

"Shoot." I said, grabbing a pad of paper and a pen from my briefcase.

"Okay, where to begin. Kid's real name is Jason Wayne Carter. For our purposes, he's been admitted as Timothy Basil. He's 10yrs 11 months and 4 days old today. Came from detention in Jefferson County, the hard core adult solitary confinement unit. Initially, they said for his own protection. Later they confessed they didn't know what to do with him. I guess when the lawyers all got together they decided he should come here."

"Why here? Why not take a team into the detention center."

"Well, I'm guessing that one thing on this kid's side is the GAL, Tom Barrows."

"Oh yeah, that explains it. What do we know about his family?"

"Lots of that is a mystery at this point. I think you'll have to do some digging, but what we do know is Timothy lives in a small bungalow in northeast Lakewood. According to case worker…"

"He has a case worker?"

"I'm guessing it's because of the criminal charges, but she seemed to know a fair amount about him."

"Oh. Okay, there's a place for me to start. Tell me

about the parents?"

"Lives with mom, some siblings-not sure how many or how old. Dad is in town, but only periodically in the picture. Sounds like a chronic alcoholic, can't hold a job, sometimes homeless. Mom has a live in boyfriend. I have no idea what the relationship is with Timothy and boyfriend."

"How about school?"

"Interesting you mention that. Apparently lots of absences. Sounds like the caseworker was considering filing truancy charges."

"Better late than never?"

"No shit. Once again, the system fails kids. I know Addy; it's because they've made so many cuts. Nobody can do that job justice."

"Okay. Stop with the administrative crap."

"Fine."

"How did he settle in last night?"

"Actually, he did fairly well. Came in, had some crackers and milk. Slept well until about 4 a.m. when he woke up sweating and startled."

"Okay. Who's his primary?"

"Sorry Addy."

"No. You wouldn't do that to me."

"He's the best we got."

"I know, but that makes it so damn complicated for me."

"I know. Just put on your professional hat and mind your boundaries. You'll be fine."

Susan didn't give me a chance to comment.

"You ready to get started?"

"I guess."

"Oh yes, one more thing. Hugh wants us all to interview him tomorrow at 2:00 p.m."

"Great. Carl's going to love this. You owe me."

"Yep. It's a list that just keeps on growing."

Susan escorts me to the south end of the unit. I realize that the brown paper is not about construction, it's to protect our boy's privacy. Susan knocks and we walk through the door. Oh Great, I should have prepared for this. Brady is with Timothy Basil; he is his primary staff member. We exchange quick glances and Susan bails me out.

"Take a break Brady, Addy will be in here for awhile."

"Sure. Hey kid, she is all right, you can tell her some stuff."

Timothy struggles for words and finally blurts out "I want him to stay."

I have to get control here. "Hi Timothy, my name is Addy. I would like to understand more about some of the things that you like to do in your free time and what your favorite soda is."

"Why? You got a cooler on you lady? Is she for real dude?"

"Hey Adrianna, me and Timothy have been talking a bit. Timothy maybe you could tell Adrianna some of the things that you told me."

"I thought she said her name was Addy, what's with the Adrianna thing?"

I realize that this kid is retreating. He is pulling inward with his body language. Timothy now has his arms crossed over his chest and is pacing around the small table where we are sitting. His affect is blank. He is appearing anxious.

"I will be meeting with your mom tomorrow, anything you want her to bring to you?" This got his attention. Hopefully a comforting thought. He begins to bite his fingernails, actually only his thumbs, one then the other. He is silent and thoughtful, almost entranced.

"Timothy?"

No answer. He stares blankly at the floor.

"Timothy?"

I think through my next move carefully.

"Jason"

"Yeah, sorry man, what were we talking about? You gonna get me a soda?"

"Sure I will. Now how about we start with some stories about you, while Brady here gets you a soda of your choice."

Timothy, Jason, whoever this kid is, will be more than a challenge. I am going to have to be more creative and back door most of my questions. I go to give Susan a "thanks a lot" look as the door is shutting behind them. Brady and Susan make a graceful exit, now it is up to me to get this thing going.

"So, you live in Lakewood?"

"Yeah, so?"

"Oh, I just wondered if you ever gone fishin at Sloans Lake?"

"Oh man, I tried that stuff, my mama don't like me smellin like fish. My dad smells when he comes home sometimes and Mama says it's why she kicks him back to the streets. I don't want to be on the streets, so I try to smell good. Hey, you guys got cologne here?"

"Well, Timothy, we have clean showers, good soap

and deodorant. Do you need more than that?"

"Maybe some privacy, you guys all watch me all the time. My Mama ain't gonna like that."

"Tell me about your mom, you seem to be very fond of her."

"Fond of her? What's fond mean?"

"It means you like her."

"Oh man, she's my Mama. That's all."

"What about the rest of your family?"

"Ok lady. Why all the stupid questions. My lawyer says not to tell anything to you people."

"I understand. Are there things that you would like to tell me?"

"I like my freedom. That's it. Oh, and my space."

"Guess you haven't had much of either of those lately."

"You ain't kiddin lady Addy."

"So, what's your house like?"

"A regular house, busy with different people, doin different things."

"Oh yeah? Who stays with you guys?"

"I got two little sisters, one three and one five, my older brothers and sisters are sometimes there and sometimes not. They really don't like Dewayne."

"Who's Dewayne?"

"Oh, mom's boyfriend. I think. They fight a lot over us kids bein around. He don't have a job, so he moved in."

"Do you like Dewayne?"

"He's better than my real dad. Leaves my mom

every time another baby comes out."

"Is Dewayne nice to you?"

"You know what? I ain't gonna tell you nothing about that night, so you can give it up now."

"No, actually I don't want to know anything about that night. I just want to learn more about your life and feelings before that night."

"My life is . . . . was great."

"How about school? You like school, got friends there, do ok with grades?"

"No, No and No."

"Well, Mr. Timothy, do you like to draw?"

"Who told you?"

"Nobody, but I will take that as a "yes" and maybe I can pull some strings to get you some art supplies. What kind of materials do you like to use?"

"Really, you would do that for me? I would love some paper and that gray stuff like chalk. And some of those colors, not like crayons, but like soft, oh, I don't know."

"You mean charcoal and pastels?"

"Maybe that's what they are called."

"Ok, I will work on getting you some of this later today. I will meet with you tomorrow again and will be seeing your mom."

"Ok, where is the guy with my soda? He said that he was coming back. You gonna leave me all alone?"

"No buddy, I bet he is right outside, just didn't want to interrupt us. I'll get him. See ya."

The parking lot was far less crowded than the weekdays. I climb into my Suburban, wondering if I will ever drive a normal car again. Visions of a two seater dance in my head. Back to reality. How am I going to tell Carl that I have agreed to take this case? Maybe I can minimize the seriousness of it so that he does not think of the stress factor. I will make an extra effort to be home on time and be very attentive. I will still be able to keep my promise to either take the family to the beach house, or to go to Ashley's tennis tournament. I will make next weekend very special, what ever we choose to do. Damn that Susan anyway. I could not say no to her after what she had been through. We would make a great team and the kid needed our perspective.

The leaves were bright green on the trees that lined the driveway. I love spring. The birds were back and singing, and the garden beckoning for my attention. I decided that since nobody was home, I would run to our local nursery and indulge in a few annuals to fill my containers. This is always therapy for me. I generally feel very productive and appreciate the work that I have done. I will change to my gardening attire and beg Grouchow to ride along. He is great company, loves to see the sights and never barks. And the good thing is if I forget to lock the car, he is my automatic security system. Nobody would dare go near him without asking.

Our local nursery is full of so many fun things. Not just plants, but wonderful handmade trellis', candles, wind chimes, garden art and more. The owners are committed to local artists and seem to attract the best. The prices are still reasonable and the hospitality factor high. Mmmmmm, I breathe in the wonderful aroma of fresh flowers. I grab a cart and suddenly become very ambitious. Through the humid indoor area, to the covered outside space that holds annuals, my nose leads the way. Pansies are always hearty and colorful. I choose a multitude of colors, and fill two flats. Next, I get some variegated Vinca vine. I finally find the Spikes and move on to the Nicotiana. This is actually a Tobacco plant, but is fragrant and blooms all summer. It is great for height in containers. I decide that the New Guinea Impatiens will be a nice addition to the grouping and will create a flow downward. I need the texture of a Salvia, and choose the orange and yellow varieties. Satisfied with my choices for the day, I move to the perennials. This is where I could really go crazy! The owners of this nursery come from a long line of botanists and arborists. They take pride in carrying rare species. I decide that some new Lavender is in order. I will not only cultivate this in my outdoor retreat, but will share some of its relaxing effects with the family as a garnish for this evening's hors d'oeuvres.

  I drag myself out of the live area, promising myself a treat from the botanical shop. This is an area that I frequent when I am looking for something really special, usually a gift. Today I will search for something that can add to my confidence and sense of ability to manage all that lay ahead. I entertain calming teas and bath salts, books on daily meditations and CD's. Nothing is hitting the spot. Disappointed, I head to the checkout counter. Oh, of course, a fresh bouquet of flowers. I choose Kniphofias, better known as Red Hot Poker as a center to work from, and Lilies for their boastful appearance and scent. This gives a full look to the arrangement already. I find a fern that offers a nice backdrop of greenery and some Astilbe to top off both color and texture. I grab some fine strands of ivy to drape their way over a vase and move quickly to the front of the store. The checkers know me by name, and give me a warm look. Absorb this, I tell myself, because this may be your only positive response this weekend.

  Unloading is never as fun as loading. Still no sign of the family. I might as well load up the loot in the John Deer and head to the back for some planting. I will decorate the patio and set the tone for a nice family dinner. Grouchow, is clearly not as motivated. He is parked by the tractor, hoping that this will not disturb his afternoon rest. I head for the gate, never hearing or seeing the family arrive. One hour and 45 minutes later, I am famished, dehydrated and filthy. I pull my tired body to the back, lower entrance. I hear music. The kids must be home. I remove my shoes and go in.

Rubbing my forehead with my shoulder, I see myself in the reflection of the artwork across from me.

I am sure that they all knew that I was here. They saw the Suburban in the drive, probably with the back still open. Why are they not at least coming out to say 'hello'? I will maintain my positive outlook while driving the tractor back to its home base. I have a wonderful meal planned and a fun evening together.

"Hello?" I seemed to be speaking to the walls, because nobody would answer. Then I see a note on the counter. It reads: "We went for a bike ride, didn't want to disturb you". Actually this is ok with me. Now I have time to take a shower and prepare a nice meal.

"Come on Grouchow, you are my shower guard." He reluctantly slugs his way to the master suite. Oh, a shower makes everything seem to come into perspective. I suddenly realize that I am not so worried about telling Carl and the kids about this new case. I have a confidence that now stems, not from flowers in a vase, shower gel, or the lovely aroma of my new lavender, but from the intensity and mystery of Jason Wayne Carter.

My lovely meal is almost complete when I hear the crew return.

"Hey mom, we went on an awesome ride."

"I can see, you all need a shower, anyone hungry?" Carl came over, smelled the kitchen and gave me a quick peck on the cheek.

"Tell me this is your famous lamb chops with the works."

I gave him a pat on the behind, I always liked him in biking shorts and sweaty.

"Ssshhhh you will ruin my surprise!"

They all scatter and prepare for the evening.

The table looked lovely. Candles added to the ambiance that already seemed to permeate the room. It seems like so long since we had been together as a family. Carl had his casual wear on. He knew that his Polo jeans were a good fit. I loved to see him look so human. He wore the cologne that I bought him for our anniversary: Ralph Lauren, Romance. I have always been in love with Carl. He is everything that I have wanted. He is very romantic, and sensitive, yet has difficulty putting him in my shoes. I could just never get enough of him. We were so in love as a young couple. We made time for each other. We had nothing. Our expectations were low. Then came the white collar climb. Carl has the perfect persona. He was recruited by the best. Our relationship changed. My role was to be that of a housewife. I tried to fulfill this. There was no way. I needed to be an equal, a wife and a mother. I have a profession. I need to work.

It was time. I thought that I would address the subject lightly.

"Wow guys, I am so proud of all of you. You are all doing so well in school and in all of your activities. My only complaint is that we all don't get to see enough of each other. Speaking of that, I have to run in tomorrow for a quick interview with Hugh at the Mount."

There, it was out, and not as difficult as I thought.

"Uh Mom? Did you forget what tomorrow is?" Jonah was always good for a dose of reality.

"Oh, sure it's Mothers Day. I guess that I had forgotten. The good news is that Hugh will not want to be there long and my guess is that he will be running the show."

"Mom, we had surprises planned for you, please don't go to work."

Jacob could really drive a hard bargain, his sad face was enough to make me call Susan and tell her I quit. The conversation would not have been complete without Jackson piping in.

"Well, you can either spend the day with us, or we disown you as our mother."

A smile began to creep across his face, and his attempt to rescue me was evident.

"What time do you have to go in honey?"

"That's part of the problem. He wants us there at two in the afternoon. I suspect that it is working around his church schedule or maybe brunch with his family. Look guys, I know that this is hard to understand, and that I promised that I was going to slow down. But this kid is in need of a good, fair assessment. I am afraid that some members of the team might not be thorough enough in my area of expertise. Besides, I am also trying to help Susan out."

"Oh, now that is a change. Haven't you, we all, done enough for Susan mom? It seems that whenever she gets you into anything, it turns out to be some hellish nightmare."

"Now Jonah, that is not fair. Susan was not responsible for any of the things that happened. She was doing what any good mom would do, and Dad and I both agreed to help." Carl decided that he had heard enough,

"Honey, why don't we talk about your idea for next weekend?"

"Well, how would you guys like to take off a day or two from school and head to the beach house for a few days?"

Dinner was so nice. We all let our guard down and I felt whole again. As I was cleaning up, Carl approached my with a very passionate kiss. He held me close, the smell of him made my heart race. He broke away, yet still had his arms around me.

"I don't think that I have ever seen this look in your

eyes Addy, you really are juggling a lot. This case seems to be quite important to you."

"It is Carl, I can't really put my finger on it, but something is not right. This is very high profile by the way, so keep an eye out for anything unusual."

"I think that we should go discuss your worries in private, you do seem a little tense." This was Carl's way of flirting; he gives great massages and has always known that I am a sucker for a body rub.

We made love for hours, the kids were on their own with movies and Gameboy. We were quiet most of the time and finally I had to break the silence.

"Carl, do you think that we could have drifted apart because we both went into a protective mode? I mean, we have been through some tough times, but never anything that threatened us like. . ."

"I know honey, let's not rehash this now."

"Oh, and thank you for sticking up for me tonight at dinner with the work thing tomorrow, it felt like we were on the same side again."

"We are."

And with that we fell asleep.

CHAPTER SEVEN

Jason - Sleepless Night

I like to draw. I'd like to draw all night so I don't have to go to sleep. These people like to see my drawings. I don't know why. Sometimes when I draw I feel like I'm dreaming, but when I look down I see these faces. They're kinda... well, I don't know. I don't know where they come from. Wonder where that nice lady is? The one who got me this stuff. At least the person in here now doesn't make me talk. He just is sitting there reading a book.

I'm hot again. Can't close my eyes or I'll see it again.

"Ewwwwww. What's that smell? Is something burning?"

"Yeah. I smell it too. Sometimes when we make popcorn, it burns a little."

"Hey, man. I got to get out of here. I can't breathe too good."

"Not so quick Timothy. You seem a little upset. Come here buddy. You're all sweaty."

"I can hear him. Do you hear it?"

"Hear what, buddy?"

"Somebody's crying. Is that a cat or a person? Please let me out of here."

"I think you might be hearing a little of the movie in the day room. It's just a movie. I don't hear anyone crying."

"Don't touch me."

"Okay. I'm just going to walk over here in the corner. I'll sit next to you, but I won' touch you."

"No man, I said stay away. Leave me the hell alone, asshole."

I'm sitting down. I'm laying down now. I'll be okay. I'm safe. I'm safe. Rocking helps. I just won't close my eyes. I just won't close my eyes.

CHAPTER EIGHT

Susan- Mother's Day

Not only do I have to go to work for my seventh day in a row, I didn't even realize it was Mother's Day. Of course, Joshua, David, and Megan remembered. I was awakened with a breakfast in bed and three yellow roses. The kids made me pancakes and bacon and a glass of milk. How they remained so sweet over the last few years was a mystery to me. It was moments like these that reminded me of my priorities, and I wondered as I drove to work if those priorities were shifting.

When I arrived, Hugh and Addy were already there. The tension in the nurse's station was palpable. If looks could kill, Addy's would have mostly certainly ended my life.

"Good morning, Nurse Kiley."

"Good morning, Doctor O'Neal, Addy." I hated these formal exchanges with Hugh. I was on a first name basis with all of the other psychiatrists on the unit. But Hugh was from the east coast and maintained these formal traditions.

"Shall we get started ladies?"

"Would you like to lead this interview?"

"Of course."

"How can Adrianna and I best support you?"

"Well, definitely don't interrupt me. But if you think I might be missing a detail, go ahead and jump in."

"Do we have an update from last night?"

"I'll check with Ellen. She took report this morning."
"Hey, Ellen can you give us an update on Timothy Basil?"

"Sure Susan. Apparently our VIP had a fairly quiet evening. He thoroughly enjoyed the art supplies you gave him Addy. You'll want to take a look at his drawings. Disturbing at best. He did have trouble at bedtime. He got hot, sweaty, and almost disassociative. Staff questioned hallucinations. He reported hearing a baby cry or a cat cry. After that, he rocked himself to sleep in the corner and wouldn't allow staff anywhere near him."

"Okay, great, thanks, shall we get going ladies."

Addy commented, "Thanks Ellen, I'll talk with you further about staff's observations."

I always appreciated that about Addy. She valued staff observations and opinions. I wished Hugh did too. As we were walking down the hall, Hugh in an accusatory tone said to me, "Who authorized the art supplies?"

"I did. His caseworker told Addy that he was a surprisingly good artist and I thought he might open up with art and I thought…"

Hugh interrupted and said, "We are not treating this child as special in any way. He is here for an evaluation, not art therapy. Are we clear?"

"Yes, Dr. O'Neal." Great way to start a case I thought to myself. I glanced at Addy and she acknowledged the same without ever saying a word.

Hugh had suggested that we set up a table for the three of us to sit at while we interviewed Mr. Basil. I asked the staff to set it up per Dr. O'Neal's request. When we got to Timothy's room, I looked at Brady. Brady nodded and I knew it was set up to specification. It looked like a small court room, with the three judges sitting next to each other. I was dismayed, but kept my thoughts to myself. Hugh sat in the middle and arranged his yellow pad and folders so that he would have easy access to them. He invited me to sit to his right and Addy to his left. We did so without comment.

"Well hello, young man. My name is Dr. O'Neal. I am a psychiatrist. I know that is a big word, but it just means that I am a doctor who talks to children about their feelings. Will it be alright for me to talk to you about your feelings?"

"Yeah. Sure."

"So, it seems a lot has happened lately."

"Listen, mister. They told me not to talk about that."

"Who told you that?"

"My lawyers."

I interrupted Hugh who seemed to be walking down the wrong path. "That's right, Tim. You can talk with us about your friends, family, and school."

"Yes. Tim. Your lawyers are right, but I want you to understand that the things you tell me, rather us, are confidential."

"What that means Tim is that when you tell us things we can't tell anyone else. But it is important for you to remember that we will be sharing what you tell us with the court," replied Addy.

"Yeah. That's what my lawyers said."

"Okay. Now that you understand the rules, let's talk about you," stated Hugh.

"What do you want to know?"

"Well, let's start with basics. How old are you and what grade are you in?"

"I'm 10 and I guess I'm in third grade."

"You guess?"

"Well, I miss a lot of school so they kept me back a year."

"When was that?"

"Maybe it was when I was in second grade."

"Okay. Do you like school?"

"It's okay."

"What's your favorite subject?"

"Art"

"Oh really? What kind of art do you like best?"

It occurred to Addy and me at the same moment that if we had waited until this interview, Hugh could have taken complete credit for getting Timothy art supplies. The brief look between us said it all.

"I like charcoal and the colored ones. What are they called again Addy?"

"Pastels."

"That's right, pastels."

It warmed my heart to see this kid's eyes light up when he talked about art. It also was a good sign to see him engaged with Addy; her ability with children was amazing.

"Do you have any of your work here?" Hugh asked.

"Oh, I doodled a little, but that's it. Maybe I'll do some more later."

"Okay. I'd like to see it if you'd be willing to share it with me."

"Sure."

It was interesting to watch this child engage with adults. Clearly, he had developed a relationship with Addy. And now he slowly was engaging with Hugh. I consider this a strength for a child. He doesn't seem to indiscriminately attach; nor does he maintain his distance at all costs. Timothy is able to let people inside his world. He's not the easiest child to read, but he has some skills. Of course, I'm the eternal optimist of the bunch. We'll have to see how this develops.

"Do you have any brothers and sisters?"

"Yeah."

"How many?"

"Are you talking about the ones that live with me?"

"Well, I guess I'm talking about both."

"I live with my two younger sisters and my baby brother." Timothy looked away for a moment. I thought I saw his eyes tear up.

"Well, I used to live with my baby brother."

"Are you talking about Russell?" asked Hugh.

"Yeah, but I can't talk any more about Rusty."

"Yes, that's right. How old are your sisters?"

"Well Mary's seven and I think Miranda just turned four. I'm not sure."

"Did you have a birthday party for her, is that why you remember?"

"No. Mama says we aren't allowed to have birthday parties."

"Why's that?"

Well, we are Jehovah Witnesses. We don't celebrate those things."

"Oh. That must be hard sometimes."

"Not really. Mama keeps me home from school on days they have parties. And it's easier not to celebrate birthdays. That way we don't feel poor."

"Is that what your mama says?"

"No. Mama says its cause the Bible says so."

"Oh. Okay. So, do you have any other brothers and

sisters?"

"Yes. But they don't live with me and mama. They're older."

"Okay. Tell me about them."

"Well I have a brother that's sixteen, and one that's about twenty, and another one who's a year younger than him. And then there's my sister and my other brother Bobby. Sometimes Bobby stays with us and sometimes he doesn't."

"What do you mean by that?"

"I mean sometimes he stays at my house and sometimes he stays with his friends."

Timothy looked at Hugh as though he were not quite right. It was amusing to see this kid take on the chair of the department.

"Oh. I see," replied Hugh, looking back at Timothy acknowledging without words that he realized that he should have understood the first time Timothy talked about his older siblings.

"Wow. You have lots of brothers and sisters." I said trying to inject a little relief into the awkward moment.

"Yeah. Mama says we are blessed that way."

"Do you feel that way too?" asked Hugh.

"I guess. Sometimes it just seems like a lot to pay attention to. Especially for Mama."

"Yes. I guess it is."

The interview continued like this for another half hour. I was surprised that Timothy was able to tolerate this litany of questions. Perhaps he enjoyed the attention. Perhaps he was hoping to impress us so that we would say good things about him to the court. I didn't know. I just knew that there was a little boy whose fate was going to be determined by a few of us. The burden seemed to be getting heavier.

I was glad when the interview ended. Hugh, Addy, and I met briefly and shared our initial impressions. Adrianna commented on his ability to engage and was anxious to review the information Social Services already had about the family. I reflected on the religious affiliation of the family. I've often thought there is a direct correlation with the number of rules in the religion a person chooses to the feelings of having little or no control over their emotions. In other words, people who feel out of control in their lives often choose religions that have excessive dos and don'ts. I think it's amazing that God provides us so many ways to seek His guidance. I will keep that thought to myself. Hugh wouldn't appreciate it in the slightest. Hugh was less verbal and it worried me that he didn't share much except the obvious: chaotic household, too many children, not enough school. Hugh seemed to be distancing himself and I wasn't sure what that meant, except I was certain it would mean complications.

While I had only been in that interview for about an hour and one half, I felt as though I had been working for about three days. I felt sad and sick for this child, for his mother whom I had yet to meet, and for a dead baby. At the same time I as irritated with Hugh. He was always so damn stiff and formal with everyone. I could never penetrate the veneer to get to the man. I wondered how he managed to become the chair of the department. Oh he was published, and had done lots of research. He apparently had gained notoriety for his work in the area of conduct disorder. Of all the diagnoses in the DSM IV, it was the one that I disliked the most. And while I had never read any of Hugh's work, perhaps this was one of the reasons I disliked working with him. Conduct Disorder is a diagnosis that basically suggests that some children simply like to get in trouble with the law for no reason— bad boys or bad girls, although boys are by far more likely to get the diagnosis than girls.

I decided to do a little work before returning home in hopes of allowing this contamination to melt off of me a little before seeing Josh, David, and Megan. It was Mother's Day after all and they had acknowledged me in such a sweet way. They deserved to have a mom who was in the present, paying attention to them and not preoccupied with work.

I went to my office and checked my voice mail and email. This would save me time on Monday. Some days it felt like all I did was respond to emails, voice mails, and my pager. I also decided to call Leanne and give her an update on the case.

"Hello."

"Oh hi Leanne, I didn't expect you to answer the phone. I figured Craig and the kids would have kidnapped you somewhere for Mother's Day."

"Well, close enough. They took me to the nursery and indulged me with all my favorites, then we came home and planted all day. Now they are making me Chicken Parmesan and a fresh green salad."

"Ohhhh. That sounds very nice. Well, I won't keep you, but I did want to give you an update on the case."

"So how are things going?"

"I think our patient settled in well. We've kept him separated from the other kids. Hugh, Addy, and I have conducted the initial interview, and so far, knock on wood, I haven't detected any media lurking around."

"How is the staff doing?"

"I think they're doing remarkably well considering the circumstances. Brady is the primary. I've heard a few comments about staff's own children and some disparaging remarks about a child that would harm a baby. I've been trying to allow for processing, but this is clearly a tough one."

"Yes. I would agree. I came in last night to check in as well. Nights were pleased to see me and they talked at length. Lots of emotion."

"What time did you come in? I must have missed you."

"It was late, probably around 10 or so. You know, I just knew the staff would need some reassurance so I figured I'd pop in."

"Well, I wasn't aware that you came, but thanks. I'm sure staff was pleased to have the additional attention."

"Yes. Oh the family's calling. Time for dinner. I've got to run."

"Enjoy. I'll see you tomorrow."

"Okay. Bye."

I wish it didn't bug me that Leanne had come to the unit, but it did. I always felt like she was checking up on me. It was clearly in her domain to make sure I was doing a good job, but sometimes I felt as though we were competing. She had been the interim clinical director until I was hired and staff had come to really like her style of leadership. She is very outspoken and upfront. She has also been in the institution for fifteen years. The circumstances of my predecessor's departure were vague and shrouded in secrecy. Leanne told me that she stepped in to help heal the staff. She also felt that I would do a good job since I was more nurturing. I guess sometimes I just wanted to be allowed to do my job. The unit didn't need two mothers.

CHAPTER NINE

Adrianna - Revelations

Delving into Social Service documents was something that I was used to. This was definitely not my favorite part of my work, but very necessary. I have always believed that it is important to look at the whole picture when assessing an individual's mental health issues. I was originally a Psychology/Pre Med major. I went into medical school and realized that physicians were very specific in their focus. The psychiatrists that I worked with began to focus on the physiological aspects of mental illness and seemed almost to disregard the psychosocial component. It was then that I realized that I was not being true to myself. I was immediately accepted to the University of Denver Graduate School of Social Work and never looked back.

Time to put my skills to the test. I had received "The Confidential File of Jason Wayne Carter" at the house yesterday, delivered via courier, my guess one of the on call attorneys for the Department of Human Services. The binder was at least four inches thick. Well, this is diagnostic in and of itself. The family has had a long standing history with the police and Human Services. Upon opening the initial documents, I felt a chill go through my body. Photographs of arms, faces, legs and torsos with welts and bruises lined the inside cover of the file. I would need a refill on my latte for this.

Returning to my home office, I decided to shut the French doors that were so infrequently used. Our house was a place of comfort and not secrecy. Now though, I wanted to shelter my family from what I was about to discover. The clock chimed, 9:30 p.m. already. Where had the day gone? The kids and Carl were wonderful. They were so tolerant of the fact that our day was interrupted by my visit to The

Mount. When I returned home, they picked up right where they had left off. They had surprised me with some new exotic plants in our lovely perennial garden near the pool. Planting them together had been their plan, but they compromised and did the dirty work themselves. They had showered me with hand made garden stones and a rare garden gnome from Ireland. Fresh tea and scones from our local bakery were awaiting me on a table near a chaise. I had to believe that my interlude with Carl had a motivating effect on him to make today extra special. I felt like a Queen.

The first section of the Carter file was MEMBERS OF FAMILY. I began to review the list. There were eight kids total. Our patient was right in the middle. There was a boy age 22, a boy age 20 and a girl age 19. They had all left the home. Currently living there was a boy age 16, Jason (our patient) age 10 years 11 months and 4 days to be exact, a girl age 7, another girl age 4, and the baby: A BOY- AGE 9 MONTHS. The only adult listed as "residing in the home" was Melinda Carter. This was the biological mother of all eight children. All eight children were reported to have the same biological father. The final sentence of this section was disturbing: "Mr. Carter appears to remain a peripheral part of this family. He is currently not living in the home and has not done so consistently for the past eight years".

Section Two was information on HOME ENVIRONMENT. Jason Wayne Carter apparently lived in a middle class neighborhood in a four bedroom house. There were two bathrooms and a small kitchen. I tried my best to picture the residence with what little description was given. It sounds like the garage may have been converted into two bedrooms. The one intruding thought I continued to have: this is a tiny house for so many people. The other was, who shared bedrooms with whom and how were these kids managing bathroom time? I wondered immediately about boundaries.

I decided that I needed to dive into reports that had

been made, and the past investigations that had taken place. I guess I was ultimately looking for more information on the specific conditions within the house. It did not take me long to see a consistency in the findings. The house was described frequently as "uninhabitable, filthy, putrid, rancid smelling, foul, rat infested, unsafe for any living creature." There were photos of piles of dirty dishes, moldy food on counters, insects inside a refrigerator, worn and badly soiled carpet and bedrooms with nothing but a stained mattress. I flipped back to the pictures of the bruised body parts. What in the world was going on in this home and why, with all of this information, were these kids still in this home?

At this point, I needed to work on looking into relationships within the family and if there were any convictions regarding abuse on the children. It appears that Mom and Dad were at one time married. The records indicate that they were legally divorced eight years ago, but he is the confirmed father of both the seven and four year old girls. They obviously continue to have intimate relations. I began to wonder how this occurred and if the children were aware of this. Was this under duress or did she consent? Why, if they continue to be together at a distance, were they not still together? A thought hit me. If he was convicted of felony child abuse, then Human Services would have required a formal separation to allow Mom to keep the kids. They could therefore justify a treatment plan to help her out as a single mother.

Sure enough I found numerous counts of child abuse, ranging from 1st degree assault to driving while intoxicated with a minor. For each child there were allegations and most seemed to involve Dad being intoxicated. There were some suspicions of the older children physically harming the younger ones, but this seemed to have been dropped. Mom was accused and plead guilty to neglect, but stipulated to having in home services and going to parenting classes. There was also mention of numerous other men, and allegations of prostitution were raised but unable to be confirmed.

I would definitely need to gather collateral information from Mom and Dad, and extended family. This family was primed for family secrets and who knows what else. I would need to interview mom, and quickly. I would also like to complete my impressions by interviewing Dad myself. I could make a call to a friend with the DA. They could pick Dad up on an old warrant and hold him at Denver Cares for the night. Denver Cares is basically a drunk tank with some empathetic staff and medical care. If I caught him at the right time, he might be willing to divulge more information. I would really like to meet with the older siblings and attempt to get their side of the story. I guess I will have to remind myself that this case has the limitations of not only time, but the constraints of Ward 1A.

I looked up for a brief moment to see Carl staring at me with very tired eyes. He was smiling in a subtle way.

"You disappeared."

"Sorry honey, you were all into the movie and I thought that I could get some work done on this massive file."

"I love to watch you work."

"How long have you been standing there?"

"Not long enough."

With that, I put down everything and was happy to join Carl in another intimate evening.

Morning came too early. Grouchow was determined to get my attention by repeatedly butting me with his wet nose. I love this dog, but the sun is not even much of a thought in the sky. I reluctantly let him out the back door and pour a fresh cup of java. I decided to get an early start. I put a call into my friend at the District Attorney's office. They were early risers. I would leave a message and Charles would get back to me by the time I was in the car. I needed to interview the parents of my Ward 1A patient today. My report was due in two days. I had a full schedule today with therapy clients back to back. I would need to clear the afternoon to fulfill my role for Jason Wayne Carter.

I kissed Carl gently on the cheek and gave him a sincere 'I love you' stroke of the face. I was off. The morning traffic was already a bear. My little community has become a major suburb. I have often thought of moving again, looking for more land and a place that feels more secluded. I guess I always return to the thought that safety lies in numbers and that I have neighbors that know my profession and my history. I feel sometimes that I have built my own little neighborhood watch. I have found that the people that gravitate to the suburbs want to find a purpose and love a good story. They have all seemed to rally around us and have made our safety their personal goal.

I need to call Susan to see about scheduling an interview with the mom. I leave her a short voice mail and decide to call the unit directly. Bad move I tell myself, knowing that Brady might have pulled a double. The ringing is suddenly interrupted by the distinct tone of call waiting. I decide to hang up on the call to the unit to answer the incoming call.

"Good a.m. to you Ms. Jennings, I understand that I might be of some service to ya today." Charles from the DA's office was always Mr. Bright and chipper. He was the most helpful and thorough man I had ever met in my life.

"Charles, I love to hear your voice first thing in the morning! I am hoping for a favor. I need a 'wanted' pulled in to Denver Cares. Should not be hard, he is on the streets."

"For you Miss, anything to eradicate crime in our lovely city."

I give him the basic information on Mr. Carter.

"Thanks Charles, call me as soon as would seem appropriate."

"Will do ma'm."

I am flooded with emotions. I have clients all day, a million interviews to conduct around this damn Mount case, and my family is watching every move that I make. I will get this all accomplished, even if it does continue to raise my resting heart rate above 100.

I pull into the parking lot at my office, surprised to see so many cars this early. I thought that I had gotten a jump on the day. I hurry up the stairs trying to avoid contact with anyone else in the building. Ahh shut the door and I have a private space for at least 30 minutes. I look over my client schedule for the day, wondering who would be the best candidates to cancel. I phoned Susan again to see about meeting with the mom. Maybe I will just call the unit to see if she has a visit scheduled.

"Hello, Mount Washington, this is Doris, how may I help you?"

"Oh good morning Doris it's Addy, how are you today?"

"Oh honey, better if you tell me your smiling face will be in here today. This case has got to get wrapped up soon. The press is outside today, Public Relations are all over us thinking that someone is leaking information. It is a mess darlin."

"Well, I intend to get on this ASAP. Do you know what time the mom is scheduled to visit today? I would like to meet with her."

"Ohhhhh girl, you are gonna have your hands full with this one."

"I had a feeling. Say no more, except what time she is coming in."

"Well, Brady is the one who scheduled the visit, because he will be supervising it, so I am going to pass you off to him, cuz I am getting another call."

"Whoa wait, Doris."

"No, sorry to disappoint you, it's Brady."

Deep breath, he sounds so like his old self, playful and almost happy. I could hardly talk.

"Hi Brady, I would like to see the mom today to interview her. What time is the visit scheduled for and could someone check with her to make sure that she has some time to see me afterward?"

"Well, all business aren't you? Mom is coming in from 3 p.m. to 4 p.m. I could call her to set up a meeting with you for 4 p.m. but it might cost you."

"Oh really? I can only imagine the price tag on this one, 4 p.m. will be fine."

"Not unaffordable, just a coffee between old friends later. I get off today at five. What do you say? You could view it as a debriefing."

"Well, let's see how my time with the mom goes and if you are even still around."

"I will take that as a little more promising than a flat out 'no'."

Great, now I can attempt to get through a hectic day while daydreaming about Brady. I have ten minutes to clear my afternoon schedule. I will leave voice mails and worry about rescheduling later.

Three-thirty rolled around quickly. I am grateful to be leaving and very excited to see Brady. I know that I am in one of those spaces where almost anything could happen. I didn't understand it, Carl and I were actually doing well. I check my hair and makeup, (what little I wore) and decided that this was very adolescent. I needed to be professional and to go in with my mind on this case.

Doris was just leaving as I was walking up to the unit. We exchanged hugs and I made a quick trek to the nursing station. It was 3:55 p.m. Good timing. I would use the office at the end of the hall to meet with mom. This was vacant for those of us who were only contract staff. The walls were stark white and the only furniture was a small round table with four chairs. This seemed to set almost an adversarial tone.

"Hello Adrianna, I would like you to meet Melinda Carter, our new patient's mother."

For a brief moment, I could only look at Brady. He looked great! Well rested and the sparkle was back in his eyes.

"Good afternoon Mrs. Carter, I thought we could talk for a bit in here. Please, have a seat. Thank you Brady." He winked and left without another word.

"Well, what is this all about? More questions, honestly, you people are the nosiest folks."

"I'm sorry if this seems intrusive Mrs. Carter, but we all have your son's best interest at heart and need to be very thorough in order to help him. I will try to make this as comfortable as possible for you."

"Well, Jason did say that he liked you. You are the one who got him the art supplies. He sure did not like the older gentleman that talked to him yesterday though."

While this waif like woman spat out insults, I noticed her appearance had some inconsistencies. Her clothing seemed to suggest that she was refined and at least middle class, though they were wrinkled and worn in areas. Maybe she shops at second hand stores. She was weathered looking and had sad eyes. I guess that I would too if I was in her shoes. Her jewelry was cheap and costume-like and her perfume very strong and sweet smelling.

"Mrs. Carter, may I call you Melinda? I think that we may get through this quicker without so much formality."

"If you must, but I bet you that I am definitely your

senior, and where I come from elders dictate what happens, not kids."

"Thank you. Now let's begin with you just telling me about Jason from the time that you were pregnant with him."

"Oh, now look here, I have eight children, and I don't remember details too well. I don't see the relevance of this to what has happened to my Jason."

"I am sure it is confusing. But I am trying to help Jason the best I can and would ask that you allow me to conduct this interview in the way I think best."

I was already starting to get aggravated with this woman. She is extremely controlling and defensive.

"Well I may just walk right out that door young lady; I will not be talked to like that."

"Oh, Mrs. Carter, I am so sorry if I have offended you. Let's start where you feel comfortable. What would you like to tell me?"

"Huh, well, Jason is a good kid. He likes to help me and he is real sweet. He reads his Bible and lives the good life. You know his daddy is not much of a role model, and has a bit of a drinking problem. I always tell the kids though, 'he is still your daddy and you need to see him as the head of the household'. Jason gets real upset when he comes to the house. He tries to defend me and doesn't like it when Nicky, his daddy, lays a hand on me. Bless his little heart."

This woman was . . . something about her affect, she was almost daydreaming about her son. It was disturbing.

"Mrs. Carter, are you saying that your ex-husband, Nicky? (she nods in acknowledgement), is at times physically abusive to you in front of the children?"

"No, I would not say abusive, just demanding, and you know, when he wants to have his way with me."

I gave her a puzzled look.

"Oh come on, you know, when they want to go into the bedroom."

"Aren't you and Nicky divorced?"

"Sure, on paper, just because those nosy social workers threatened to take my kids. Nicky gets carried away sometimes and believes strongly in discipline. He had a couple of times when he was driving with the kids after having a beer or two. Once married, always married and it is my duty to serve him."

"I see. Do you ever get angry about these 'duties???'"

"Comes with the territory, Jason understands the good life and sacrifices that we all have to make."

"Does Jason enjoy any activities outside of the church?"

"Of course, he is a normal child. We have a basketball hoop and he likes to draw, he plays with the animals at home and helps out with the little ones."

"You have pets?"

"The kids have dogs and cats, a prickly thing that lives in a cage, had a turtle and some fish."

"Wow, sounds like a full house. Pets are a good way to teach children about responsibility."

"Oh, Jason understands responsibility alright, since the older kids are grown and mostly gone, Jason is really the second man of the household."

Just then the door burst open, it was Brady.

"Mrs. Carter, Jason would like to see you, he is very upset and says that he needs to tell you goodbye again. I had feared that you were already gone, I am sorry about this intrusion, there was no sign on the door."

"Well, Ms……"

"Call me Adrianna please."

"Sure, Adrianna, we will end our little talk now. I hope that you will not need me for anything further. I am very busy."

With that Mrs. Carter sauntered down the hall. I noticed that she was wearing very high heels. That seemed rather odd. I began to gather my things, this bizarre interview had me lost in thought. I almost felt physically ill. The door closed and Brady stood in front of me smiling.

"What?" I could not keep a straight face either. The chemistry between us is intense.

"I miss you Addy. I thought all day about this moment and all I want to do is hold you and kiss you."

"Oh Brady, you know the risks are too great for us to do this all over again."

He was moving closer and the room was already small enough. Before I knew it, I could smell his scent and he drew me close. Our kiss was passionate and still held so much emotion.

"Brady"

"Shhh, just allow me this for a couple more minutes."

We held each other and were both teary as our embrace ended. He kissed my eyelids, a romantic gesture that was unique to him. I knew that he still loved me. I could not let this happen again.

"I'm sorry, I have to go."

He slowly held my face in his hands and wiped away my tears.

"I know."

The spring air helped me pull myself together. It was rush hour and I was just leaving downtown. I decide to get rid of my guilt by touching base with Carl.

"Hi honey, I am just leaving downtown and wondered if you would like me to pick up something for dinner?"

"You are coming home early tonight? And what are you doing downtown?"

"Oh, the Mount case, had to interview the mom, I am fried and need some down time."

"Addy, how about a night out, just the two of us? We can order pizza for the kids. I know that Jonah is planning on being home, he can watch the twins."

This is not what I had in mind, I was actually hoping to get them all fed and take a bubble bath and fantasize about Brady. I realize that this is not healthy and that a date with my husband is exactly what I need to get back on track.

"Oh Carl, that would be so nice, where should we go?"

"It will be my surprise. See you at home within the hour, maybe we could grab a quick shower to freshen up?"

All right, that was enough, I could not even think about even kissing Carl right now.

The kids were fed and taken care of. Carl dressed in business casual, smelled wonderful and was being the perfect gentleman. I was trying very hard to respond, but the case was weighing heavy on my mind and I could almost feel Brady's lips on mine whenever thoughts of him intruded on my evening.

"You seem preoccupied tonight, is it the case?"

"I'm sorry honey, I interviewed the mom today and it was probably one of the creepiest discussions of my career. I can't really put my finger on it though. I am going in tomorrow to look through the chart to get an idea of staff's impressions. Maybe that will help."

"Oh . . .is . . . never mind."

"Is what Carl?"

"No, No really, I don't want to ruin our evening, just forget it."

"Carl, don't do this!"

"Look Addy, there are going to be trust issues, the guy was in love with you. He practically stalked you."

Yeah, I thought to myself, he is still in love with me and the kiss today was so tender and loving that I want to do it again. Keep pushing me and I will.

"Addy, are you listening to me?"

"Carl, I don't want to fight ok? I am tired and stressed and just want to go home now."

"Fine, I was a fool for bringing it up, I should trust you. I am sorry Addy."

CHAPTER TEN

Jason - Desperate

"Mama, I am scared of what's goin to happen. They have been askin me all kinds of questions. I don't like to sleep at night; I have been having dreams of the night..."

"Sssshhhh! They are right outside that door. Now you listen to me, we both know that you are a good boy and that you are Mama's helper. I'm gonna get you back real soon. You just watch what you say and don't let that nosy lady get to you."

"What? You mean Addy? She and the guy Brady are the ones that I like best, and it is Dr. O'Neil that asked me if I did it."

"You didn't say anything did you baby?"

"No Mama, don't worry, remember I have been the man of the house, I know how to handle myself." The door opened, great, it's them again, no alone time with Mama, they are going to make her go now. "Mama? Before you go will you sing me the song?"

"Sure baby,

I hate watching Mama leave, because I know that she is going to go home and cry. She is trying so hard to be strong for me. I feel a kinda bad that I almost like it here. This is kind of a break for me. Its quiet and I don't have any little kids running around. I really don't have to do anything that I don't want to do, but talk. I hope that they will let me do art all night.

I want to close my eyes just for a few minutes. Man I am tired. I think that maybe I should try to remember more. The lights and the sirens scared me so much that I can't remember what really happened. Why did Mama keep having babies? There was no one there to help me. I remember that. It was the daytime and this was not the usual way that things happened, I remember that too. Mama was getting real mad. I was trying to help. I just wanted everything to be ok and I hate it when Mama gets mad. She had that look in her eyes. Shut up, shut up, shut up, please shut up.

"Hey, Timothy, wake up buddy"

"What?"

"I think that you were dreaming. You kept saying shut up and you were crying."

"Was not man, and don't be writing that down. You guys always write everything that I say and do."

"Hey, you slept through dinner, I saved you a plate, do you like corn dogs and French fries?"

"Alright. Can I do my art stuff later?"

"Sure you can, I will even teach you how to play a game called Mancala. Its fun and goes fast. Let's get you something to eat and we will see how you feel. By the way, do you want to wash up a bit? Sometimes a quick wipe to the face with a wash cloth does wonders."

CHAPTER ELEVEN

Susan - Security

As I drove into work Monday I thought about Brady's comment from Saturday, about the count being off. Three times in a month was too much to be coincidental. Ritalin is a drug that can be abused and while it is not physically addictive, one can gain a psychological dependence on it. For children with Attention Deficit Disorder, it is often the drug of choice. It has been widely researched, is remarkably safe, and can help children focus and be successful not only in school, but in many social situations. For people who do NOT have ADHD, it is a drug to abuse in order to maintain high energy, achieve weight loss, and decrease the need for sleep. I couldn't imagine any of the staff abusing Ritalin. I didn't want to be naïve, but I honestly had a hard time believing staff would: 1) think this wouldn't be investigated, and 2) think that if they were selling it that they would not get caught. I knew each of the staff on Ward 1A fairly well. I thought the staff to be of high integrity and with a loyalty to children. But this was the third time so I was going to have to investigate carefully. Besides, it was a diversion from this case. By law, narcotics are required to be counted at the end of each shift. One nurse completing his/her shift has to count with one nurse just starting their shift. Each nurse has to sign that the count is correct and all narcotics are accounted for. Part of my investigation will be to see if there is any consistency with who was counting when the mistakes were noted. I would also look at the schedule to see who was in charge and what the staffing patterns looked like as well as which patients were taking Ritalin at the time of the missing doses. I went to the nurse's station and got the narcotic book. Ellen acknowledged that I was taking the book to my office.

She said, "I know the count was off again. I really

can't figure it out."

I said, "It's disturbing. I'm going to try to figure out what's going on."

"Boy, you really need the count to be off right now with this case on the unit."

"Well, it's kind of a nice distraction. I can focus on numbers and signatures instead of sad stories for a moment."

"Way to put a spin on something, Susan," Ellen smiled.

"Thanks. It's my area of expertise," I chuckled as I walked to my office. I poured over the narcotic log and the schedule. I listed every staff member on duty during the shifts when the count was off. I couldn't see a pattern. I found two instances when one staff person was on, but not on the third. As I sat focused on my lists, the phone rang. It was an outside call.

"This is Susan."

"Oh hi, Susan. I expected to leave you a voice mail. Long weekend, huh?"

"Oh. Hi Jon. Yep, it was a long one. I can't believe that it is Monday already."

"Happy Mother's Day a day late," he said with that soft melodious voice that made me melt.

"Thanks, Jon. The kids woke me up with breakfast in bed and three yellow roses. Man, am I a lucky lady or what?"

"I'm so glad they did that for you Susan. We took Elaine to brunch Sunday morning. I think she liked it but, you know she wears out so easily now."

"I'm sorry, Jon. That's got to be so hard for you and the kids."

"I didn't call to have a pity party for me, Susan.

How's the case going, missy?"

"It sucks."

"Would you like to say more about that Nurse Kiley?"

"Not really. Addy, Hugh, and I interviewed our young patient yesterday. I wish I didn't have bad feelings, but initially I felt like Hugh was trying to get more information from this kid than he should have."

"Oh, really? Like what?"

"I don't know. Like alluding to talking about the incident. Addy set good limits on that. And you know, he just doesn't connect with kids."

"Susan, maybe he's just trying to maintain some professional objectivity, unlike some people I know."

"Okay. Okay. I know I let my emotions get into my work, but I'm objective. Just not cold and icy." Jon chuckled when I said that. He knew I wasn't fond of Hugh or his work and he often chided me about my responses.

"So, how's the rest of the unit doing?"

"Funny you should mention that. The count was off again, so I'm gazing at the charts I've made trying to identify a common thread. It's not happening."

"What a mess Susan. What are you going to do?"

"Well, I've notified you. That should be enough."

"Seriously, Susan." His voice changed and I knew I'd better have a plan.

"Okay. Well, I'm looking at the staffing and the narcotic book. I'll get creative Jon. And I'll make sure it doesn't keep happening, okay?"

"I know you're working hard, but I don't need this kind of crap just as I'm leaving. I want to make a clean break. Surely, you can understand that."

"Yes Jon, I do. I promise to give it as much attention as I possibly can right now." As much as I adored working with Jon, he could be irritatingly right. I always felt like I was about twelve years old during those conversations and that I should say, "Yes father." Fortunately, he didn't do it often and most of the time I was able to understand that he was right.

We said goodbye shortly after that interchange and I decided to work a little differently on this issue.

I decided to call George Sanchez, the chief of security at Mount Washington. George was about 5' 7" and had a muscular build. He had short salt and pepper hair and sported a mustache. He had been named the Chief of Security about a year ago and was doing an excellent job. He had made some changes in the security department and staff commented on how much safer they felt. George had extra lighting installed in the parking lot and he had been instrumental in helping the hospital pick out a new, recently installed, video surveillance system. Not too long ago, the system identified a young woman who was coming into the hospital, stealing purses, and running up huge credit card bills within hours of the purse snatching. Because of this new system, the woman was apprehended and charges were brought against her. While I'm not sure George can help me with this, I'll see if he has noticed anything unusual when he makes rounds.

"Hi Susan, what can I do for you?"

"Hi. George. I was getting ready to leave you a detailed voice mail. You're never in your office."

"Generally that's true, but I just happened to be working on time sheets."

"Thanks for the reminder. I've got to get those in too."

"I'm assuming you didn't call me to discuss time sheets."

"Sorry. I'm so distractible right now. I have a problem I'd like to discuss with you in person. Can I come down?"

"Sure, Susan. I'll be waiting for you."

I went to George's office on the first floor and sat down. I told him how the count had been off three times, how I had looked at the narcotic log and the staffing plan and how I hadn't been able to identify any commonalities. I asked him if he had noticed anything unusual this last month when making rounds.

"No. Can't say that I have. Staff seems pretty much the same. Of course, everyone is a little on edge right now. I assumed it was because of the case."

"Yeah. The case isn't helping, but this has been going on for a month."

"Well, I do have one idea. You know that video surveillance system we have?"

"Yes."

"Well, I have the capability of installing a hidden camera that looks just like a smoke detector. We could place it close to the narcotic cabinet to see if anything is going on around there. My only request would be that you not tell anyone else, except maybe Dr. Hollingsworth and Dr. O'Neal. I'll let Judith know." Judith was the vice president of Clinical Affairs.

"I had no idea you had those capabilities. I actually think it's a good idea. Do you have policies in place for this kind of thing?"

"Yes, we sure do. I drafted them about six months ago and they were signed by the higher ups just a few weeks ago."

"Wow. I worry about the impact on staff, but I absolutely have to get to the bottom of this. It's bad enough to have this high profile case right now, but to add this to the mix is just a mess."

"I know. But I do think this is the quickest way to get to the bottom of what's going on. Don't you?"

"I suppose," I replied. I can't really think of another way to get to the answer sooner."

"I'll have my assistant install it tonight. I'll have him tell the staff that there's a problem with some of the smoke alarm indicators in our office and that they are just checking to make sure they are working properly."

"You've got it all figured out, don't you George? So am I the first one to get to use this handy little addition to the new security system?"

"As a matter of fact, no you're not. We've already been observing some unusual things in another area of the building. Of course I can't tell you much more than that." George winked at me and I knew not to ask more, but I also knew that at some point, he'd likely figure out a way to tell me all about it without saying a word.

I notified Jon and Hugh of the plan when I returned to my office. They both agreed to keep things very quiet. I sat in my office pondering the last few days. I needed some time away. Psych is one of the toughest areas to work. To have to look at staff in a similar way made me unsettled. Once this case was over, I'd take a week off and pretend like I was a 'stay at home' mom. Some of my favorite times away from work were just staying at home and devoting my day to kids, cleaning, and a quiet kind of life. I loved it, even if it was only for a few days a year.

CHAPTER TWELVE

Adriana – Spencer

The sunrise is beautiful. The temperature today is supposed to be in the 70s. I really need to spend most of the day at the office. I will head to the Mount after I finish with clients. It will make for a long day, but at least that way I will avoid Brady and will be able to concentrate on reviewing staff notes in the chart. Carl has already left for the day, not a good sign. I wonder if he is mad at me, or himself. I will try to call him later to smooth things over. First I need a shower.

"Grouchow, come on buddy, its time to rise and shine. Hi big guard doggy, watch my back will ya?"

Client wise, Tuesdays are one of my more enjoyable days. I have a lovely couple who come in first thing. They are struggling with a number of issues, but mainly some infidelity. They are very insightful and so willing to work. They have been consumed with young children and have given little time to their relationship. I actually think that they may be happier now than ever before. They are working on better, more direct communication and meeting each other's needs. This is such a typical scenario. Our society dictates that monetary success is what we should use as a measuring stick. Young couples are primed to accept this, and so wanting to impress their partner they lose sight of the intimacy.

My next three appointments are with children in foster care. They are a sibling group and have just had to say goodbye to their birth parents. The Department of Human Services actually made a gallant effort to help these parents pull it together. They are both addicted to methamphetamine and continue to manufacture and sell the poison. The kids, ages 5, 6 and 8 were all taken into custody during a drug raid on the home. Their trauma is severe and they may never be able to attach to an adoptive family. The foster family is wonderful and very well educated. They have successfully raised two children of their own. I am hoping that their level of attachment to these children will lead to a willingness to adopt them.

At noon, I have to run to a working lunch with two attorneys to work out a potential parenting plan for a divorcing couple with four children. This should be a real treat. They are both very reasonable and have assured me that their clients 'want what is best for their children', yeah, I have heard that one before. I will try to return voice mails during my short drive to and from lunch and otherwise put off calls until my commute into the Mount. My late afternoon is the ugly part of my day. I have to meet with a father and teenage daughter who have become estranged through a divorce. They are so much alike that it is hard to make much progress. He is intrusive and she is just plain stubborn. This session usually drains me. I will have to find some humor today to get through.

I dial Carl's cell phone, hoping that he is going to answer. I am actually not even sure where he is. He has been traveling less, trying to "be more available". I am the one who has distanced now and still have some resentment that he waited so long to pay attention to his family vs. work. No answer, he may actually be traveling. I guess I will leave a voice mail.

"Hi Carl, I am sorry that we weren't able to talk things through last night. I was tired and should have been more sensitive. I love you. Please call and let me know where you are. Bye."

I realize that if Carl is out of town and I am going to be home late that I need to check with Jonah to see if he can pick up the twins and throw on some dinner. I text message him, so as not to interrupt him during school. I should hear back from him within the hour.

Lunch was actually refreshing. The attorneys worked well together and had their presentation organized. This was more of a consultation, but they would now like to file a motion with the court that I become the parenting coordinator / arbitrator on this case. I reluctantly agreed, not really wanting any new cases right now. Upon returning to the office, I get a call from Carl.

"Hi honey, did you get my message?"

"Yes Addy, I was glad to see that you actually called, but after I listened to your message, I felt like there was not much use in even communicating with you anymore."

"Excuse me? I thought that I conveyed my apologies quite well and made a nice effort at moving forward."

"Which is fine and good, but you seemed to completely forget that your husband was traveling across the country and that you have a family to attend to. I am in New York. Remember that conversation or were you once again 'focusing on your work?'"

"Carl, I know that you want to blame me for all of this, but if you remember, you were the one gone so much that your family did not know if you were coming or going. You are just as guilty of putting your energy into work. I am preoccupied right now. I am also running my own business and raising our kids. So get off your high horse and stop with the finger pointing. When are you coming home?"

"Is that your idea of moving from arguing to 'moving forward to a solution based discussion?'"

"I am done talking Carl. Mimicking me is not productive and you are still trying to punish me. I will see you whenever, until then, I will make sure everything here goes smoothly."

With that I hung up. If he only knew that this is the very behavior that drove me away in the first place.

My therapy day is finally over. I am wiped out.

Traffic into the city is flowing well. What a gift. I may actually get home to see the kids before they go to bed. The parking lot was emptying out. The nine to fivers packing up and heading home. Doris was gone and the unit preparing for dinner. I grab the charge nurse and ask for Timothy's chart. It was locked up in the Narcotics cupboard. I decide to head to the unit classroom. My only other option for privacy is the office at the end of the hall and I did not need the memories of Brady right now. I quick check in with the kids.

"Jacob?"

"No mom it's Jackson. When are you coming home? Is Daddy with you?"

"No honey, Daddy is in New York again. I will be home as soon as I can. How was your day?"

"Mom, can you tell Jacob and Jonah to stop bossing me around. They are being really mean."

"Jackson, let's try to get along. Do you have homework?"

"Yes Mom. How are we supposed to get to hockey? Or did you forget that too?"

"I am sorry honey; look at it as a night off. Put one of the brothers on the phone. Love you."

"Hi Mom. Where are you?"

"Hi Jacob, are you picking on Jackson?"

"No", he lies," where are you?"

"I am at the Mount, finishing up on a case. Get going on your homework and listen to Jonah, no hockey tonight and get in the shower soon."

"Ok, Dad says that he doesn't like it when you go back to the Mount. How come?"

"We will talk later sweetie, put Jonah on. Love you."

85

"Hi Mom, yes I have it under control. Do you want me to take them to hockey? Jackson is really upset about missing it."

"No Jonah, I know that you must have homework and your own thing to do. How is Ashley?"

"Great, see you when you get here mom."

"Thanks Jonah, I love you."

There were copious, detailed notes from the staff on our new felon. The team was doing an excellent job of charting just the facts, no impressions. They were well trained by Susan. She has such a nice way of working with everyone. They have never turned on her, which is amazing in psych. I scoured the pages for patterns in observations. I did note Timothy had a more difficult time around visits from Mama and bedtime. He fought sleep and seemed to get almost disassociative. This was common for children who have suffered trauma and basically meant that their brains took a vacation at times when they felt threatened in any way. They were generally not responsive and would almost look drugged. Our little guy was not on any medication and he was found to be physically healthy, but had a number of residual scars. His eating habits seemed normal for his age and he seemed to be very quick witted. The staff did note that he would become tangential, and his thinking became fragmented at times. One example that really seemed to be pertinent is when staff was playing a game with him. Timothy was apparently day dreaming and staff prompted him by saying "your turn".

Timothy quickly replied, "The door handle turns and doors open, open wide Mama says when she feeds the baby, babies cry, Mama cries."

"Hey Timothy, buddy? It is your turn in the game, you want to go?"

"Oh right, sorry." It did appear that our patient was at times borderline delusional. He made frequent comments that were grandiose. This means that he seemed to believe that he was superior to others and in some way exceptionally special.

I would need to talk to staff specifically. The notes reflected quotes from our young man, but no opinion from staff as to whether Timothy seemed to really believe these statements. There are many times that people say things, especially when they feel threatened. They develop a defensive posture that can be misconstrued by others. I had to be careful in my investigation of all of this information and cautious in my impressions.

My concerns about our team began to grow. I had left the Mount for a reason and my ethics were gnawing at me again. Hugh should not be on this case. He is very research oriented and his area of expertise is Conduct Disorder. This was beginning to feel like a set up. Hugh also has a six month old baby boy. How could he be objective? I was beginning to regret taking this case. It was a never ending. I was also beginning to have concerns about the psychology and testing aspects. Gene is the head of the psychology department and always a kiss ass with Hugh. They were both heads of their department, but ultimately Hugh had more power. Gene has always been concerned about job security and I had the feeling that he would do whatever he had to, to keep his position.

I closed up the chart and headed for the nurses station. The team was busy getting the patients settled for evening meeting. I gave the chart to the charge nurse to be locked up and asked for Timothy's consistent staff on evenings. I was directed to his isolated area and noted that as I walked in, there was an extra person in the room. Timothy noticed me first and said.

"Hi Addy, come here and meet my big brother."

Hmm this was new, I thought. I had not heard that any family members other than Mama had been to visit. A flash of "what if" went through my mind. How did staff know who this was? What if this had been someone from the press? We know now that there had been no leaks to anyone about Jason Wayne Carter's whereabouts, the press was bluffing to see if we would cave.

The young man stood up and moved toward me with his hand out.

"Hi, I am Jason's second oldest brother, Spencer." His handshake was firm and he made eye contact. The wheels in my brain were spinning. This seemed like a gold mine. Would this kid talk to me? I may find out more about this family tonight than I had thought possible. Great, my report was due tomorrow. I would be up all night. At least Carl was gone.

"Nice to meet you Spencer, I am Addy. I am the Social Worker involved in this case here on the unit."

"Oh" He said with a half smile.

"You must be someone who has had one of those 'very positive experiences with Social Services!' I am not that kind of social worker."

"Sorry, I am just a little leery these days."

"Quite understandable Spencer. Would you like to find a space to talk?"

"Sure, I guess so, but I don't really want to hang around here too long, you know?"

"I'll let you two say goodbyes and I will grab a key to an office off the unit. I will meet you at the nurse's station."

I begged staff to have security open Susan's office, knowing that she would not mind. Again, this was for the kid. I had to protect this brother's confidentiality. We sat a bit awkwardly at first. He was rambling about the difficulty with the bus system and evening hours. I decided to be direct.

"Spencer, I could not help but think that you wanted to tell me something other than your woes with RTD buses. What's on your mind?"

"Well, you have to agree not to tell anyone that I told you any of this. I don't want them after me."

"Who are them?" I asked with a quizzical look. Spencer was very uneasy, avoiding the question, he began.

"Ok, here it goes. I figure that it is time to spill the beans to someone and now that Jason is in this far, I have to say something."

I wondered at that point if I should have a Denver Police officer present. This kid could be opening a can of worms and anyone would be hard pressed to get him to testify. My testimony of this conversation would be considered 3rd party information and would be all but thrown out.

"Spencer, wait, do you think that you should do this for the record?"

"You mean get the cops involved? No way will I do that. It's either me or you, or I walk now."

Breathing heavy, I take a quick look at my watch.

"Would you allow a staff member to join us, so that if this ever needs to be verified that we have a witness?"

"You got someone that you can trust?"

"Sure do, give me a minute." I broke away quickly to search for staff that would be up to this task. Of course, just my luck, I run into Brady,

"Hey, I need you for a few, would you come with me?"

"Well, Adrianna that was really forward now wasn't it. And to admit the need part, what is that about?"

"Look Brady, it's all about business at this moment. Clear yourself from the floor, we are in Susan's office with the kid's brother."

"Ok, Spencer, this is a safe place to talk and we want you to take your time. Tell us everything that is on your mind."

"Well, I have been gone for a long time. My older brother is 18 months older than me and it started when he was 14. He ended up in one of these psycho places too. But he was way worse. He was whacked out man, on lots of medicine. He was in restraints and shit. They messed with his mind."

"Do you know why he went into a place like this?"

"Yeah, my old man is a drunk and used to hit us. He hit him more than me. He didn't like our noise and the fact that the mom had to pay attention to anyone but him. One day my brother went to school and could not sit on the chair, my dad had whooped him so bad it was bleedin. The mom did nothing, and told the school that he fell on the bonfire while camping. She always made excuses. My brother started to talk more and was threatening to tell. My dad was furious. He started saying that my brother was crazy, hearing things and seeing things and making things up."

"So they lied to get him into the hospital and your brother was so mad that he acted out and got himself on meds and in restraints."

"Yeah, pretty much. They never let him come back home. He went to a group home and then ran away. He is messed up still."

"How about you?"

"Oh, well. I stayed as long as I could. I learned to be quiet and watch. I stayed until I started to see things that I could not be quiet about. I had no choice but to leave, or have the same thing happen. I thought that because she liked him, he would be safe. "

"Liked who Spencer?"

"Jason, she treated him special. He was her baby boy. Dad was so sick by then, he was not so much of a threat, he would just come home to have sex with her and leave again. Man, and was I ever stupid. I thought that all along, he was the problem. It is her."

"What do you mean Spencer? I thought that your dad was the abusive one and that you all suffered from that?"

"You could see the abuse from him; he is just a stupid ass drunk that played with a sick bitch when he could. She manipulated him too."

"I am sorry, I still don't understand."

"Look, she tries to look normal, says that she goes to church and all. Well, she has to be the center of attention and I mean the center. She would make my dad beg to see her naked, he would grovel and cry. Then she would kick him out on the streets. She would come out of the bathroom and let her towel fall off in front of us and then scream at us her religious bullshit. She would say that we were evil for looking at her."

"I would scowl and look away, but Jason was too young to understand. She had him in her grip. I thought about taking him with me when I left, but was afraid that I couldn't take care of myself, let alone him. Now I wish to God that I would have taken him. My dad has helped me out. He is not such a bad guy. He's just stupid and drunk."

"Spencer, do you think that there is abuse going on in your home currently?"

"Wow, have you heard anything that I have said? It must be a social worker thing you all want to believe that it is the guy that does the bad things. Like I said, you could see the stuff that Dad did, the mom was so much worse and the fact that you can't see it makes it perfect for her."

"What else goes on at the home? Are there drugs? Other men? Are there religious rituals?"

"Bingo, now you are starting to get it. All but the drugs. She is a puritan remember. The religious stuff is so twisted man. She is like brainwashing the little ones. I almost think that Rusty is in a better place. He will never have to deal with her."

"How often do you see her and the family?"

"Never, this is the first time I have risked coming out of the woodwork, and it's only because I love my little brother. The sad thing is he does not get it. He is so suckered into her ways, but I can tell, he likes it here. He is glad to be away, but won't say so."

"Spencer, this is all very disturbing, why won't you go to the authorities?"

"Simple lady. She said that she would kill us all. I gotta go; the buses are hell this time of the day, any time of the day for that matter. Hey, thanks for listening and please help Jason."

Spencer was gone and Brady gave me a long look. He was very sincere and said "You ok?"

"Oh sure, just putting some things together. Did you notice that he kept saying 'the mom'?"

"Yes, I did what was that about?"

"Well, he has depersonalized her to the point of using a qualifier to identify her. He obviously has no use for this woman and feels that she is powerful and destructive."

"Aren't you all?"

"Damn it Brady! This is serious. I am not in the mood for your callous jokes. I am working really hard to keep my alliances to my family and you just don't........."

At this point a hug was exactly what I needed, though knew that again I was crossing a line. He held me tight, slowly and tenderly stroking my back. I was breathing heavier and did not know if this was because I was about to cry or was feeling aroused. I started to speak and he immediately put his fingers to my lips.

"Ssshhhh, I know. Just take some deep breaths and let go of it for now."

Why did he have to be so empathetic and comforting? Carl would do this if he thought it would get him a little, but this is why I was attracted to Brady in the first place. He was human. We stood there for what seemed like a long time. My phone began to ring in my purse, this broke the silence. I pulled away and dried the tears that had been streaming down my face. He very quietly took my hands and looked into my eyes.

"I love you Adrianna, our lives are separate, but I will always love you. Please know that I am here and that it is on whatever terms you want. I have always been your friend first and your lover second. You do what you need to do, but know that I am here for you."

I had an urge to kiss him at that point and to let him hold me for hours. "No," I thought. Fight this one, you have to start somewhere.

"Thank you Brady, I appreciate your support. I'm also glad that you were here for this interview. I may need to chat about it some more. I am going to put some thoughts on paper and will go from there. Have a good night."

I drove home, trying to clear my thoughts. I realized that I could not let our trip to the beach go by the wayside. We could do a full week. Yes, this is exactly what we need. I decide that there is no better time than the present to call for flights. Delta had nothing into Norfolk until Monday the 23rd. I was hoping to leave on Friday, but this will have to work. Actually, this way Jonah can have the weekend with Ashley and we could start our time together in Beaver Creek at her tennis tournament. I will have a glass of wine and relax when I get home. I am thinking that this case was more than I had bargained for. How do I get myself into these messes anyway? Thanks Susan!

CHAPTER THIRTEEN

Jason – Shelter

"Hey, Brady?"

"Yeah kid?"

"Do you like working here?"

"Why do you ask?"

"Don't know I kinda like being here. Does that sound weird?"

"No, not considering where you came from."

"Do you like being married?"

"Who said that I was married?"

"Well, you're wearin a ring. Don't that mean you are married?"

"For a kid, you don't miss much! What do you think about being married?"

"No way. I am going to be by myself when I am old enough. I want to do my own thing. Ain't nobody gonna tell me what to do."

"Being married is more than telling the other person what to do. It is a partnership, someone to share your thoughts and dreams with. Like a best friend."

"What? That ain't what I see."

"Really, what do you see?"

"Never mind that, want to draw with me?"

"You would share your stuff with me?"

"I guess so. You any good?"

"I used to be in high school. I haven't really taken

time to draw in awhile."

"Did you see my brother?"

"Yeah seems like a nice guy. You see him often?"

"Never, he has to stay away. Mama would kill him."

"Really?"

"Yeah, probably, she says that he is bad and that he does not know the Bible. She says that about a lot of people. Do you think that my brother is bad?"

"I think that he cares a lot about you to risk coming here to visit you. He says that your dad drinks a lot."

"Oh, my mom says that too. She still has him come around though. But she always kicks him out real quick. I don't get it, but I ain't supposed to ask. Mama says that it's adult business and it is sinful to snoop. What do you want me to draw?"

"Well, you always seem to have dreams, you talk in your sleep and wake up really out of it, why don't you draw something from your dreams? You may not dream it anymore if you get it out on paper."

"You think that would really work? I can't really draw any of it though."

"Maybe if you just start and see where it goes. I am going to grab us a snack, you ok in here for a minute?"

"Sure."

I really like this guy. He seems to care about what I am saying. Should I tell him anything? No! My lawyers said NO! I will not let anyone hurt me and if I let them get inside me, they will hurt me. I will not, but I feel different here. I feel safe and like nobody's going to touch me. I still know that I am bad, but they make me forget that sometimes. I like the quiet and no other kids here. I like that lady Susan, but why do her eyes get watery so much. The lady must really be sad about something. She maybe has had something bad that happened to her too. Maybe I will ask her. She seems safe too. I am done talking to the moron guy - Hugh. He was really an idiot. He either treated me like I was two, or he hated me and wanted to hurt me. I am glad that guy is not coming to visit anymore.

"How is the drawing coming?"

"Oh, I guess I was spacing out, I haven't started."

"What did you say that I should draw?"

"Anything you want buddy, it's all good."

This guy is cool, his smile is nice and he is not pushy.

"Got you a snack, do you like those big warm pretzels with cheese dip?"

"I can try it, probably won't like it though. Hey Brady? When do I have to go back? They told me I would have to go back. Can you get them to let me stay longer?"

"I wish that I had that kind of control, I don't make the rules; I just follow them. Let's have our snack and watch some T.V."

CHAPTER FOURTEEN

Susan – Staff Meeting

The unit seemed more settled since Timothy had returned to detention. I decided to have a staff meeting to allow for feelings to be processed and to discuss some of the day-to-day activities of the unit. I also wanted to talk about the narcotic count and institute a few changes.

I found it best to have meetings in the evening. Staff working twelve hour shifts usually had the energy to come in a little early, day shift staff were generally willing to stay later, and those working straight evenings were thrilled to have a meeting on their watch. We convened at 6 p.m. and shared Chinese food. Our meeting space is a large playroom that is located at the extreme north end of a long hallway where patient rooms are located. It is a good space to meet since it is close to the unit, but separate enough that confidential information can not be overheard by children or their families. The playroom is lined with shelves where toys are kept. While the toys are often well loved, they are organized so that play can be easily accessed. Children are encouraged to play with the toys and art supplies. A part of play time is clean up. Children must help the adults to clean up after every play period. In this way the children learn responsibility and the play area is ready for the next time. Lots of hard work happens in the play room. Children are amazing at their ability to work on very difficult issues during play. Seasoned staff are able to acknowledge children's work and share important observations.

I decided to start the meeting discussing business. I reviewed the quality improvement activities we were currently working on and praised staff for continuing to collect the important data we were required to maintain. We talked about staffing schedules and I asked staff to look at the empty spots to see if they wanted overtime. I then shifted to the narcotic count. I explained how the count had been off three times in the last month. I also made sure staff understood that this was being taken seriously and was being evaluated closely.

"Has this ever happened before?" asked Emily.

"Not for the five years I've been here," I remarked.

"I worked at a place one time that had that happen. They finally figured it out and set up a situation where the person would do it again. Sure enough, this dip shit walked right into it and did it again," Mike tells us.

"Then what happened?" asked Amanda.

"Fired his butt and reported him to the Board of Nursing. His license was revoked after a trial. Oh yeah, he spent three solid years behind bars," continued Mike.

"Damn. They joke, but they don't play," added Brady.

"Glad I don't have a license to lose. I don't envy you guys that have to put your license on the line everyday," stated one the mental health counselors.

"Bigger paycheck. Lots more risk," said one of the nurses.

"It's one of the reasons I like working in psych better. Psych is just plain tighter than other areas about stuff like this. This kind of crap happens in ERs and ORs all the time. I know it can happen anywhere, but psych units are so tightly controlled by JCAHO and the state. It seems like it happens less here. Plus, you work psych for a little while and you wonder why anyone would want to abuse drugs."

"I have to agree with that," stated Amanda.

"I appreciate your comments. If anyone has seen anything unusual or wants to discuss this or anything else for that matter, please come see me. If you can't find me, please page me. I really am available 24 hours a day, especially if it means that this issue can be resolved. And if for some reason, you are involved with this in any way, please contact me as soon as possible. I don't want to spend a lot of time on this today, because we clearly have other pressing issues to talk about, but I honestly want to say that if someone is involved with this and comes forward independently, I will make sure that we treat this as carefully as possible. There are many resources for health professionals to get help. There is a great peer assistance program for nurses in the city. I know one of the leaders of the program and I will make sure that this is treated extremely confidentially."

I paused for a moment to let that sink in. I hoped that if one of the staff was involved with this mess, they would choose to come forward and get help rather than force me to seek criminal prosecution. The Board of Nursing would have to be notified. It would be much better if there was a nurse seeking help, rather than a thief being caught. I would have to wait and see how this sorted out. After a few moments I switched topics to the hardest of all.

"I wanted to thank you all for hanging in there this past week. I know it's been tough to hold on to all the feelings."

"No shit, Susan. How did we get this catastrophe anyway?" asked Ellen.

"Unfortunately the court ordered him here. I suspect that part of his admission here was related to the court's attempt to give them some time to figure out where he belongs."

"I can't imagine how scared he must have been in detention. It took him a few days to settle once he was here," Brady supported.

"But it didn't make sense to have him here. I mean he is charged with murder. How could we make other kids feel safe with that?"

"That was one of the many reasons we decided to keep him separate from the other kids," I felt myself getting defensive. I generally try to become more subdued when I feel myself like this. It's a good technique so that I don't interrupt the process and allow staff to talk freely.

"I know Susan, but this is a baby killer we're talking about," Mike commented.

"We don't know that for certain." Thank goodness for Brady's help.

"I have a baby at home right now. I could barely look at him," Mike added.

"I appreciated you asking not to participate in his care, Mike. Not everyone is so aware of how those kinds of circumstances can impact feelings." I wanted to support him. He was an excellent counselor and that awareness is to be commended.

"I have three kids. One of them is Timothy's age and one is a toddler. I couldn't imagine Brian being brutal enough to hurt his brother much less kill him. Nevertheless as a mother, I wanted to care for Timothy. I had a hard time imagining what his life must have been like to get him to that point; assuming the charges are true. I wanted to experience him and make sure my own kids are protected from whatever led him here." Amanda's words silenced the group. I let them sit with the quiet for a few minutes. I, too, had felt Amanda's emotions.

After a few minutes passed Brady spoke, "Thanks for saying that Amanda. I've been sick all week thinking about this child, about the situation. I think you've captured the torn feelings we all have. Some of us with babies, some of us with our own middle schoolers. This is a tough as it gets. They are both victims."

Sometimes the most poignant comments are made during staff meetings. It's a time for staff to come together, dig into issues, small and large, and share. This staff is amazing. I thoroughly respect the depth of their work. They made it easy for me so many times, and while today was just one example, there were many more.

CHAPTER FIFTEEN

Adriana – Unfinished Business

Report writing is one part of my job that I loath. I love to put things together, to wrap my head around information and come up with an impression or understanding of someone's life from a psychosocial standpoint, but not to write it down. I have so much information that has loose ends that this one is going to be a challenge. I will start by jotting down some things that seemed to have links to pertinent information. I need to help the court understand the life that this child has led and is leading. I need to put the pieces together for myself too. Let's see, no special education services needed, not even for behavioral problems. He has been a suspect in illegal activity, but never convicted. Dad is an alcoholic and has been convicted of child abuse. One older brother was removed from the home through a sketchy hospitalization, and this seems to be related to his reports of dangerous and abusive behavior at home. The other older brother is by choice and through fear, estranged from the family. This party reports that mom has been rather elusive. She sounds like she is potentially emotionally, and mentally very abusive, and that religious and militant rules govern her home. Will have to look into this one further. I guess I will have to work with what I have and can always file an addendum with the court later.

DEPARTMENT OF PSYCHIATRY AND BEHAVIORAL SERVICES

MOUTNT WASHINGTON WARD 1A
DENVER, CO

Psychosocial Assessment

Patient: Timothy Basil

Age: Timothy is currently 10 yrs, and 11 months

Interviews and collateral information: I have interviewed Timothy a total of three times, one being a group interview with Dr. Hugh O'Neil and the Clinical Director of the unit, Susan Kiley. I also interviewed Timothy's mother, Mrs. Melinda Carter, and one of his older brothers, Spencer. I have reviewed the entire Social Services documents and have spoken with the current worker assigned by the Department of Human Services.

Home environment: Timothy lives in a small, single family home in a middle class residential area. He is one of five members of the household that live there on a consistent basis. There are also numerous people, from extended family to friends that are reported to be staying in this home at any one time. The home has been reported as "uninhabitable" due to numerous health hazards including animal and human feces on the floors, walls and furniture, a dead cat in the basement, and garbage and maggots in the kitchen. The property is surrounded by an old wooden fence that in many places appears unstable. The backyard was described as "dangerous", as evidenced by numerous rusty metal objects and old broken cars. There were apparently puddles of what appeared to be discarded chemicals, and urine soaked mattresses. There was dirt and weeds throughout and many clusters of scrub oak.

Significant Relationships: Timothy has not been very forthcoming with information on his relationships. He seems to be conflicted in his feelings regarding both biological parents. He talks minimally about his siblings and seems bonded to some, yet is guarded about others. Timothy does not talk about a best friend or any peer relationships. He appears to be quite isolative.

History of Psychiatric or mental health treatment: Timothy has no prior history of any type of mental health treatment according to reports by mother. The school records show just two visits to the school counselor for what appear to be routine matters. The Social Services documents indicate that the family refused in-home family therapy at a time when there were numerous reports made anonymously by the community. There is question as to whether there is a family history of mental health issues. Timothy's mother was very guarded and vague when asked about this issue.

Religious and Cultural issues: Mrs. Basil currently practices as a Jehovah's Witness. She expressed a strong belief that her children were to abide by these religious doctrines. Interviews with family members other than Mrs. Basil indicate that the children may feel intimidated and controlled by these religious practices.

Legal History: Timothy has been accused of criminal behavior but has never been convicted.

    I find myself wondering if I am writing this report with an agenda. I certainly feel that this child needs help. Maybe it is time to take a break. As I slowly get up, stretching my old stiff muscles, Grouchow meanders in to support me. I decide that a run with my hound may do me some good. The air is still moist from a short spring rain. The steam is rising off the pavement. I stretch and tie my shoes. Grouchow gives me the look.

    "Come on buddy, you know this is good for both of us."

    The trees continue to rain droplets on me as I make my way along the bike path. I breathe deep and try to clear my head. I know I will change my focus to our trip to the beach.

    Our beach house is in Duck, NC. This is a very unspoiled part of the coastline. Carl's family frequented this area when he was a child. When Carl's grandfather passed away, we received a large inheritance and decided that we would memorialize him by building our beach house. We knew that this would be in the family for years and designed it to accommodate numerous families as our children married and had children of their own. We have nine bedrooms and ten bathrooms. It is a Victorian style, three story home with wrap around porches on two levels. Our home is on prime ocean front property. The Outer Banks are so narrow that we also have a view of the Sound. Both Carl and I love to cook, so we went all out on our main kitchen. We have stainless steel appliances with a restaurant style Viking stove, two dishwashers and a sub-zero refrigerator. The floor is made of Italian tile imported from Rome. We decided to add a radiant heat element under this floor in particular, as it can get quite chilly in the evening. The dining area is adjacent to the open style kitchen. We found an old, rectangular, antique dining table made of wormy chestnut wood that seats sixteen. The lighting is a combination of old world chandeliers and warm wall sconces. We furnished the third floor family room with leather couches, chairs and ottomans. The window coverings are sheer to allow the sun in, but also soften the space. We of course have heavy shutters on the outside of every window to prevent hurricane and high wind damage. The family room is adorned with dark wood and boasts floor to ceiling wood beams. The family's collection of favorite books lines the walls. We have many black and white photos of the kids growing up on the beach. The family is alive in this home. Handmade throws drape the furniture to ensure a cozy atmosphere for reading or just relaxing. Our cabinets are lined with games. Tradition in our family is to have the big Scrabble play off and the marathon Monopoly game. This is truly a place where we are bonded.

  Suddenly Grouchow is running off the bike path. I am jolted back to reality. "What is it buddy?" I see something moving through the tall grass. It must have been a snake. We have had a particularly wet spring. I realize that I have completed three-fourths of my run. How nice to daydream. I will put the paperwork aside for now and will spend some time catching up on client contact and scheduling. I love to daydream about our vacation homes and the time that we spend just relaxing and enjoying life, but the truth of the matter is that I would not be able to give up my work for long. I very much enjoy the autonomy that my livelihood brings. I love the stories that I hear and the help that I can offer those in a crisis. This is a good way to end my run. Thoughts of empowerment.

CHAPTER SIXTEEN

Jason – Detention Again

"Hey, Jason. Time to get up. Remember today is the day you have to go back." It was Brady. I like Brady. Whenever he was here, he was assigned to me. He talks quiet. I like that. No yelling.

"Yeah, I remember."

"Are you doing okay?"

"I'm just fine."

"You sure, Timothy?"

"Look. I'm fine. I knew I would have to go back. Today is just the day it's going to happen. Did they say anything about where they were going to put me?"

"No, sorry bud no one has told me about that. I can ask Susan."

"Okay."

"Would you like some breakfast before you go?"

"Sure. The food there sucks."

"And this is better?"

"Yep. Sure is. What's for breakfast?"

"Looks like oatmeal and toast."

"With sugar?"

"Yes, Timothy, with sugar. Two packets since it's your last day."

"Sweeeeeeeeeeeeeeet."

"While you're eating I'll go talk with Susan."

"Okay." Mmmmmm, I love oatmeal. Sometimes

Mama makes me oatmeal. It has to be a real special day, but sometimes she does. I wish I could just go home. I just want this crap to be over. I'm tired of only talking to lawyers and having to be somebody else. Timothy Basil is a stupid name. I like my name; Jason Wayne Carter. Mama told me I was in the newspaper. They got a picture of me from my school. Mama said I looked handsome. Brady comes back with Susan.

"Hi Timothy. Remember me?"

"You're Susan, right?"

"Right. So, I talked with some people from the court today and yes, you are going back to detention. For right now, you'll be going back to the same place. But the people at the court said that once there is a hearing about you, they might be able to put you in detention with other kids. For now, you'll still be by yourself in the adult place. Do you have any questions for me?"

"What's a hearing?"

"That's when lawyers from the court and your lawyers get together to meet. They will probably also have Dr. O'Neil and Dr. Gene come to meet with them and ask them questions about you."

"Aren't you going to be there? And Adrianna?"

"Probably not. We have been working with you to help the doctors."

"That sucks. I don't like them."

"Well, it's probably not so important to like them; they are going to try to help you anyway. That's their job to help kids."

"Well, they aren't very good at it."

"I'm sorry you feel that way Timothy. But I do have some good news. Adrianna talked with the court and suggested that you be able to take your art supplies and have time each day to do some art work."

"Really?"

"Yes, really."

"Second sweet thing that happened today; oatmeal for breakfast and I still get to do art."

"I'm glad you're happy. Do you have any other questions for me?"

"Nah, but thank Adrianna for me."

"I sure will. I won't be here when the guards from detention come, so I wanted to say goodbye now. You've done a great job here Timothy. I know this is a really hard time for you right now, but I want to tell you that I've been very happy with all the work you've done. And I want you to know that my thoughts will be with you."

"Ah, thanks. I wish I could stay here instead."

"I hear you. Hopefully, the court will find a good place for you to stay. A place that will help you feel safe all the time."

"Yeah."

"Good bye Timothy."

"Bye." Susan left. She had that funny look again, but I didn't try to pay to much attention to it. I got my art stuff together and gave it to Brady. Brady said he would give it to the guards for me to have once a day. After a little while the guards came to get me. They cuffed me after I was away from the unit. I kind of feel sick. I just want this to go away. I really just want to go home. I won't tell them that. They'd think I was a sissy for saying that. So I won't. I'll just stay quiet.

CHAPTER SEVENTEEN

Susan – Subpoenaed

I finally got the kids to settle and decided to give myself a manicure before I went to bed. There was something relaxing about sitting in my easy chair, watching a little TV and filing my nails. I wondered if I was a complete introvert or if it was the fact that I had only recently been able to enjoy these alone moments that made this time so sweet. At any rate I enjoyed these quiet times and before I knew it I was deep in thought planning the next day at work.

While it wasn't terribly busy at work, I wanted to finish a stack of evaluations so I could keep Human Resources off my butt. The Joint Commission for Accreditation for Hospitals (JCAHO) dictated that evaluations be done in a timely manner; HR took it to a whole new level. If I was one day over the month the evaluation was due, Human Resources reported it to the hospital Board of Directors. Unfortunately, the unit often took priority and I was always dropping those evaluations off the very last day. The eyebrows were always raised when I came rushing over to Human Resources at the end of the day, on the last day of the month. So I resolved that today I would get to work early and get them done. I only had six to do this time and if I was organized I could get all of them done before the end of the day.

I was happy that the unit was in its summertime mode. Fewer patients, more relaxed staff, more camaraderie. It seemed that most of the staff had talked through the "unwanted visitor" and he wasn't discussed as much. No further Ritalin had been missing and I wondered what that was about. Was it the staff meeting that put someone on alert? Was it just a strange mistake that there were medications unaccounted for? In truth, it could easily have been just an unfortunate mistake and someone had wasted a dose or two without a witness. Whatever it was, I was just happy it hadn't continued. I hoped it was a strange series of mistakes; however, deep inside I found that hard to believe.

Just as I had begun to polish my nails Megan walked into my room.

"Hey cutie patootie. What can I do for you?"

"Mommy. I can't get to sleep."

"How come little one?"

"Mom. I'm not a little one. I'm your oldest daughter."

"Good point. And after all you will be going into the fourth grade this coming fall."

"Yeah, I will."

"So, what's up?"

"I'm scared again."

"I'm sorry. Come here and sit with me a while. Would you like a manicure?"

"Yes, that sounds good."

As I polished her nails, I gently asked her some more questions. I knew what was on her mind. Her daddy had died two years ago. And while in some ways it seemed hundreds of years ago, in others it seemed only a few months. Adam's birthday was July third so it made sense for her to be thinking about him.

"So, were you thinking about dad?"

"Yeah."

"Well, that makes sense. His birthday is only about two weeks away."

"And this will be the second birthday since he died."

"I know."

"I know he didn't like his birthday too much, but I liked making him cakes."

"You always made very good cakes. How about you make a cake this year and you, me, Josh and David celebrate all by ourselves. We can remember the good things about Daddy."

"That would be fun, Mommy. Josh and David always remember the bad things."

"Well, Josh and David have some bad memories they have to talk about. Sometimes I do too."

"I know Mommy. Sometimes I do too. It's just that I don't always have bad memories."

"Makes it kind of hard to sort out, huh?"

"I guess. I wish sometimes Daddy hadn't done what he did."

"Me, too. I wish that I could still talk to him and work things out."

"Me too. Mom, can you paint my nails different colors on each one?"

"Sure. You pick out the colors, and your wish is my command."

Megan was always good about letting me know when she was done talking about the heavy stuff. In a few weeks she would tell me more, but it was important to let her lead me. I had a hard time processing Adam's death myself. Fortunately I had great friends who let me explore this painful territory at my own pace as well.

Nails got polished and dried. Megan was tucked into bed and I read for a little while before dropping off to sleep myself. It was not a restful sleep. I didn't remember my dreams, but from the look of my bed I must have been having some battle. I got about up about 5:30 a.m. so I could get showered and ready for work before the troops were up. Josh, David, and Megan were sleepers. It was summer and I was fortunate enough to have an awesome college student come to the house to care for the kids.

I had just gotten out of the shower when I heard the doorbell ring. Who in the world would be at my door at this hour? I grabbed my pink terrycloth robe and headed downstairs. As I peered out the long narrow window outlining my door I saw a plump man in his mid-forties standing on the doorstep with papers in his hand. I opened the door slightly leaving the chain hooked.

"Susan Kiley?"

"Yes?"

As he shoved this envelope through the crack into my hands he mumbled, "Subpoena ma'am. Sorry." turned and left without another word.

I opened the document. Sure enough, it was a subpoena. June 23rd 8:00 a.m. Court House 4M, District Court, Jefferson County in the matter of Colorado vs. Jason Wayne Carter.

Just when I thought this wretched case had gone away, here we go. My stomach was churning. I wasn't sure why, but this caught me off guard. I made myself a cup of coffee and sat and looked at the subpoena as if it was going to change and say, "never mind, we don't really need you to testify, Susan. You've been through enough. Take the day off and enjoy your coffee." Okay, back to reality. I'd better call Addy and give her a heads up.

CHAPTER EIGHTEEN

Adrianna – Ruined Plans

I awoke to a knocking on my front door. Who could be here this early? I roll over to look at the clock, 5:45 a.m. The knocking continues and is getting louder. My household is sound asleep. Putting on my robe, I run down the stairs to the door. Looking out the window I see a short man with tussled hair and glasses.

"Can I help you?"

"Yes Ma'am, I am looking for Adrianna Jennings."

"I am Mrs. Jennings, what is your business here sir?"

"I have a subpoena for you Ma'am. I can just leave it here if you are more comfortable."

"Yes, that would be fine, and any particular reason that you did not serve me during general business hours?"

"Orders Ma'am. I am sorry to have disturbed you. Have a nice day now."

As the man turned to leave a sinking feeling came over me. In all of the years in my profession, I have never been served at home. I anxiously opened the door as the car turned out of sight. The standard envelope was secured with a piece of tape. Moving quietly through the house, I made my way into the kitchen and decided to have some tea. I perch atop a bar stool and open my mystery mail.

The 18th Judicial District commands you to be at the Jefferson County Court house on June 23rd, 2005 to testify in the matter of Jason Wayne Carter. . .

I can read no further and have become very clammy.

"Good morning early bird, see you got the worm."

"Damn it Carl! Don't do that to me."

"Sorry honey, just a friendly greeting to my lovely wife, what is it? You are not usually this jumpy."

"You would not believe this. The case that I am consulting on at Mt. Washington, well, I was just handed a subpoena from some swarthy little man at 5:45 a.m. at my own home!

"Well, it is not unusual for you to have to testify honey, and you are so good at it."

"Carl, you know this is an extremely sensitive and high profile case. Hugh assured me that I would not have to testify. Not to mention, the 23rd is Monday and we are supposed to be at the beach."

Stepping out of the shower I can see that Carl is still fuming.

"I am truly sorry Carl. What can I do? I will fly down as soon as I testify and will be in by Monday night."

"Sure Addy isn't it convenient that you just happen to have us going away and you stay here. Oh yeah, just coincidental that Brady is on the case. Think that you may be sequestered, in a hotel possibly? Away from all media and just working your little tails off?"

"That is crossing the line Carl. I told you that Brady and I are finished. Keep pushing me like this and I just might have to make you paranoid fantasies come true!"

"Any excuse Addy, any excuse."

I hate to drive when I am angry. I become so much more aggressive. Screw Carl! It's not like I am happy about staying here. I arranged the whole trip to be with the kids. I need to vent before getting to work. Its only 7:30 a.m. who can I call? Ok, just deep breaths and positive mantras. Sometimes I get more worked up when I talk about things like this. I really don't understand why he is still hanging onto the Brady thing.

Traffic is lighter than usual. I dial my office number and begin to check voice mail on the way in. Call waiting is signaling me that I have another call. If it is Carl? Answer, don't answer? What the hell.

"Hello, this is Addy."

"Addy? Can you talk?"

"Sure you really wanna go there with me today Susan?"

"Look Addy, I don't know what is going on in your life, probably a Carl thing, but we may have trouble."

"You aren't telling me anything I don't already know. Let me guess, you just had a knock at your door from some swarthy little man with mystery mail."

"Not exactly, mine was actually kind of hot and I was just stepping out of the shower, but yes, the delivery was the same."

"Sounds like the most fun you have had in a long time, did you at least put a towel around your womanly body?"

"Shut up Addy, I really don't understanding what is going on and I don't have a good feeling about this."

"Well sister, me either, but now I have bigger fish to fry. Remember the make up trip to the beach with my family? Yeah, I am basically screwed!"

"It's not your fault Addy. We were told that there was no chance that this would happen. I am certain that Hugh would not be behind this, he would not want to share the limelight."

"I agree, then who would want us there, and what the hell are we going to do about our differences with Hugh and big Gene?"

115

"Well, what is your day like today? I think we should try to get together to talk about some of this."

"Lunch? Panera's is halfway. I have clients all day, but scheduled a break from 11:50 to 1:30."

"Sounds great Addy, I will see you there."

My office is generally a safe haven, but today even my home was invaded. I need to finish my voice mails before anything else. I need to put all of this out of my mind so that I can be productive with my clients. I push the necessary buttons and hear "You have seven voice mails". Scheduling issues and calls from new clients. These can wait. My last voice mail sent chills throughout my body. "Hi Addy, this is Charles, the favor that you asked of me, to bring in a Mr. Carter, well I have him here for you. Won't be able to hold him too long. Got him on a vagrancy charge."

I was frozen in time. This is too surreal. I had completely forgotten that I had spoken to Charles, and to have this happen today was just strange. I have to get down there. My curiosity was driving me to cancel my afternoon appointments and to make a trip to see some of Colorado's finest in their favorite digs.

I dial Donna, my part time administrative assistant. She returns calls and does general scheduling and billing for me.

"Hey Donna, sorry to bother you on your off hours, but I need you to clear my schedule for me this afternoon."

"Sure Adrianna, you leaving early for the beach?"

"Don't I wish? It's a long story Donna. I appreciate your help."

"Sure Addy, see you when you get back, have a great time, and I will try not to page you with any issues."

Donna works from home most of the time. Our computers are in sync, so she can access today's client list without having to come into the office. I will pack up at 11:30 and go to the jail after lunch with Susan.

The hours seemed to drag on. I actually had a boring line up of clients today. Spoiled suburban housewives. They all think that their husbands are cheating on them and seemed to be competing to be smaller than any other woman on the planet. Their neurosis seemed to be contagious, because most of them wanted me to see their children also. This makes for a lucrative practice, but my ethics continue to win out and I refer their children elsewhere. I fill up my coffee cup in preparation for my last client. This is a 15 year old girl, a product of divorce and molestation. We have a lot of work to do.

Closing my office door always has created some anxiety for me. Though everything is under lock and key, I worry that some of my court cases could drive unhappy clients to try to break in and steal their files. I try to correct my thinking and then remember that Susan said Ritalin was continuously missing from the medication cart. Ok, double lock the door and move on. My car was extremely hot and smelled like Grouchow. He had been in there yesterday afternoon after a quick romp in the lake near our house. Wet dog and heat do not mix and definitely began to turn my stomach. The wind was nonexistent today, so air conditioning won out. I dialed voice mail to catch up on calls that came in during my sessions today. I was pretty much over my anger with Carl and was hoping that he had called. No such luck. I dialed Charles's pager, wanting to let him know that I received his message and would be there this afternoon. I quickly dialed Carl. Voice mail. I could not really find the words to say. Better to talk in person. Charles called back immediately.

"Hi sweet thing, how is my favorite head fixer?"

"Charles, you are charming as always, thank you so much for the pick up. I will be there by 1:30 today."

"Good thing darlin, somebody's called to bail him out."

"That's interesting do you know who this is?"

"No, think it is his wife maybe."

"My other line is ringing Charles, see you this afternoon."

"Hello this is Adrianna."

There was a long pause on the other end and finally Carl spoke in a very soft, rather beaten voice.

"Did you call me?"

"Yes Carl, look, I am sorry for what I said. I know that the marriage counselor said that I need to allow you to get mad from time to time and that I should not react."

"No honey, I was the one that was really out of line, I have been ruminating ever since you took this damn case. I am just feeling really insecure."

"Carl, I am so sorry. I really had no idea. You seemed to be taking this all in stride. Why didn't you tell me earlier?"

"Oh sure, like I want to lay myself out there again."

"Carl I love you and chose to stay with you, and I am really upset about this weekend, but I will be there on Monday. Can we move forward please? For the kid's sake Carl."

Panera's was crowded for a Thursday. No parking spaces. I ended up parking in the garage two streets over and wilting in the 90 degree heat. Susan was already there and had a table for us. Her face was apologetic.

"I am so sorry that I got you into this Addy."

"Hey, what else do I have to do?"

"So what the hell is this all about Susan? We were

told, no wait, you told me that it was only going to be the big boys testifying."

"Now wait a minute Addy, that's what I was told by Melissa Rubenstein, the hospital attorney."

"Do you really trust that woman? She seems so controlling and I felt almost dismissed before even starting the case."

"No shit, she is the queen of control, but rumor has it that she is really good with the corporate stuff. She not only represents Mt. Washington, but also three other hospitals in the area. Damn my pager is going off. I don't recognize this number, order for me and I will be right back."

I peruse the menu and decide to go with my usual, French onion soup in a bread bowl, roasted turkey for Susan and two diet cokes. The wait seems endless and where is Susan? I notice someone waving to me. Oh God, it's a former client. I can never escape.

"About time, are you okay Susan?"

"You would not believe who that was."

"Who?"

"None other than Melissa Rubenstein."

"What? What the hell did she want? To warn you about the subpoena? Real timely Melissa!"

"No Addy, she says that she just found out about them a few minutes ago, and get this she had the nerve to ask me if we asked to be subpoenaed."

"Oh yeah? Ok, give me that bitches number and I will tell her how blasted happy I am to miss my trip to the beach with my family and to be hanging around in court next week."

"No, come on Addy, this is getting weird, I reminded her that she told us that we would not have to testify. She got quite the attitude, and then told me the subpoena came from the defense attorney and that Hugh and Gene were subpoenaed by the prosecution."

"What? Why would the defense attorneys put us in that position? I have only talked with the GAL."

"Do you suppose that our reports reflected the split that we were feeling between us and the guys Addy?"

"Well, come on, it is natural to have different perspectives, that is why they wanted a team rather than an individual. But, Susan, we both know what happens when you cross Hugh."

"Did you ever get to read their reports?"

"Right Susan. Of course not. Hugh asked me for mine and I never heard anymore. How about you, did you read theirs?"

"No, but Hugh asked me for mine as well, and there were no copies of his report or Gene's in the chart. Your report was in and my nursing summary was in there."

"Interesting, so really we have no idea what Hugh did with our reports. You know I also talked with Human Services and they seemed to be very worried about their management of this case."

"Wow, did you hear that? This has POLITICS written all over it! This is not about evaluating a ten year old accused of murder. This is all about how the community will eventually view Ward I-A. And better yet, Dr. O'Neil. Think about it Suz, Social Services could get fried on this. Who is one of our best referral sources?"

"Oh man this is getting ugly. There are a lot of players and some really bad press. I don't feel good about this. I have continued to wonder why we got this case in the first place. You know, Hugh seemed at ease and almost excited when I informed him."

"Let's eat and be merry shall we?"

"Hey, by the way, did you ever solve the mystery of the missing Ritalin?"

"No, I had a staff meeting and discussed it at length, told all of the staff that I would make sure to get them help in the most confidential way possible. Nobody came forward, but no more Ritalin is missing either."

"Well, what do think was going on? Do you have any suspects?"

"No, I am still puzzled. I just can't imagine any of my staff doing that. Nobody has the symptoms either."

"Right, any effects of Ritalin could be disguised as type A personality, all psychiatric nurses are type A, not to mention neurotic, except for you Susan. Oh my God! I totally forgot to tell you that I am headed to the jail to see Mr. Carter after I leave my lunch date with you."

"Addy, how did you manage that? I thought that when you turned your report in that you were finished with this case."

"Ok, guess today's little subpoena changed that, didn't it?"

"I really am sorry that I got you into this Addy, would it help if I talked to Carl? I could let him know that I didn't really give you a choice."

"Thanks, I have to handle this one on my own. I am a big girl and I made the decision to do this. Listen, I gotta run. I will call you after I see Mr. Carter."

The County jail is never a fun place to visit. Our detention facility is only three years old, and has many amenities that the old one did not have. This does not change the fact that there is still a smell that permeates the inside of this place. I enter into a very sterile looking area with cameras viewing all angles, and recording every move that I make. The guard sits on a high stool, behind a U shaped desk. He is reading something and barely looks up as I enter. He points to the sign that tells all visitors to remove all jewelry, watches, keys and valuables. I am instructed to put my belongings in a plastic bin. The guard takes this bin and a small key with number 8 on it. He moves slowly to the area behind him and places my belongings in a locker. After locking this up he puts my key on a hanger and gives me a small laminated piece of paper that says #8. He gestures for me to move through the metal detector. A man of few words I guess. I make it through the detector without incident and move to the next locked door. I am photographed again, by the video surveillance camera. The door automatically opens. I then walk outside through a small area that is covered by barbed wire on both sides and on the top. The ground is cement. The next door opens and a guard meets me in the entrance.

"I am here to see Mr. Carter sir. My name is Adrianna Jennings."

"Ah, yes Ms. Jennings, I have been expecting you. Paul said that you would be by. Mr. Carter is asleep. Doesn't look like the old chap gets too many good nights sleep. I think that he doesn't really mind being here, if you know what I mean."

"Yes sir, would you kindly wake him and I will wait in the interview room?"

"Sure thing Ms. Jennings, make yourself comfortable; well as comfortable as one can be here."

As I stand to greet Mr. Carter, I realize that I am a good six inches taller than he. The smell is overwhelming. He has been in custody for about 18 hours and still smells like alcohol. His hair is dark, my guess from grime and oil. He is filthy and appears to be stained. I remind myself to breathe through my mouth, as I try not to wince.

"Mr. Carter, Thank you for seeing me. I am a therapist that has been consulted to work with your son Jason. Are you aware of the trouble that your son is in sir?"

"Well, I know what I seen on the news and what some of the guys have told me. Is he alright Ms.?"

"Yes Mr. Carter, Jason is ok. He is back in detention, awaiting a trial. I wonder if you could give me some history about Jason and even your relationship with the family."

"There really ain't much to say about me and my family. She likes to have me every now and then, you know, she is into the Jesus thing and can only have sex with me cuz we married. She is a Jehovah you know. She thinks she is always right. Pretty funny huh? I am one of those guys who gets used and tossed out on the street like garbage. Oh yeah, but I keep goin back for more. Guess it must not be that bad. Sorry ma'am, what was it you wanted to know?"

"You are doing fine Mr. Carter. Please tell me more about Mrs. Carter and the kids." "Well, ok. What is it that you wanna know? She always says that she wants to raise our boys in the 'proper way'. I really don't know what she means by that, but could be I don't do the parenting right."

"Mr. Carter, tell me about your oldest boy. I forgot his name. Spencer?"

"What? How do you know about him?"

"He came to see Jason at the hospital and he talked to me for some time sir."

"Now that was risky, I told that boy to be careful. If his mother finds out she will kill him."

"Excuse me? Do you mean that literally sir?"

"Well no of course not Ms. My wife would never harm anyone. I gotta go lady."

Mr. Carter disappeared as quickly as his beaten body would let him. I have a lot to think about. How does all of this relate to the case at hand? Mr. Carter was beaten but not crazy. He had a fairly linear thought process and was able to show empathy and concern for his children. I don't know what this man is hiding, but my gut tells me that there is more going on.

The sun was glaring as I headed west out of the parking lot. The temperature on the mirror of my car read 98 degrees. This has been an almost unbearable spring and summer. The danger of wildfires is extreme and makes hiking and camping less than pleasant. The fires have destroyed more of Colorado's forests this year than the last two years combined. We all hope for rain, but the consequences of that become further damage by mud slides. Those who manage to escape the fires without the loss of their homes continue to live in fear of moisture of any kind. Life is ironic.

CHAPTER NINETEEN

Jason – "Mama"

The guard comes to get me for a visit. I hope it's Mama. I hate walking down these halls. The men always make sounds at me. I act like it doesn't make any difference, but it does. It makes me scared. I'm sick of feeling scared all the time. Everything makes me jumpy. Will I ever not feel jumpy?

"Hi Mama. I'm so glad you came to visit me."

"Hi sweetie."

"Mama, can you get me out of here? I hate it here."

"Now my little man. You know your Mama is doing her best to get you out of here. But there's only so much I can do. The lawyers are working on it. It just takes time."

"I know Mama. But I'm so scared in here."

"Little Man. You have got to be tough."

"But Mama."

"Now that's enough. Look what I got."

Mama holds up her hand to the window. She's got some stupid ring she's flashing at me. She probably got it from Dewayne. I hate him. He's such a jerk.

"Jason. You're not saying anything. Isn't it pretty? Dewayne and I were watching TV one night and I flipped on the jewelry channel. I couldn't believe he let me buy it. It's just the prettiest thing I ever saw. I love all the diamonds. Don't you just love it Jason?"

"Ah, I guess Mama. It's real pretty. Are you spending a lot of time with Dewayne?"

"Well. More than before. You know he is good to

me Jason."

"Yeah Mama."

"I know you and he don't get along, but maybe it will be better when you get to come home. You know he has a job now."

"That's nice Mama." I don't even want to think about going home with him there.

"Don't look so sad, Jason. You know I don't like it when you look sad. It makes Mama uncomfortable."

"Sorry Mama."

Just then the guard tells us that visiting hours are over. Mama smiles at me and says good bye. I get up with the other guys and get in line to go back to my cell. Maybe I'll just stay here for a long time.

CHAPTER TWENTY

Susan - Court

Monday, June 23

Addy and I met at the courthouse an hour before the hearing. We were both nervous. I bought a grande peppermint non-fat latte for Addy and a hazelnut one for myself. We both sipped our coffee expectantly waiting for some sort of calm to overtake us. It didn't.

"So how bad do you think this is going to be?" I asked.

"I don't know. It should be straight forward. I mean for goodness sake, we just want this kid to get some help."

"I know. But I keep wondering why I feel so crappy." I knew why. It wasn't one thing. It was everything. I had been to this court house before. I had walked on the cement circular walkway to the revolving door. I had placed my pager, cell phone, and jewelry into the guard's plastic basket. I had walked through the security entrance and been asked the same questions about weapons and contraband. I hated this court. I briefly wondered why I had to come to this court again. Out of all the courts in Colorado, why here? Why now?

Addy said, "Duh Susan. It's deja' vous all over again."

"I know. Fortunately its two years later and this is work and not home."

"Yup. I agree. You know I thought the comments Melissa made the other day were weird. Seems pretty clear that the split in our views must be evident in our reports."

"I was thinking about that too. What I don't get is why she'd want to muzzle us. Like Hugh and Gene would want the kid prosecuted or something. Even if our clinical views differ, surely we all want the same outcome.

"You'd think, but it seems so shrouded in secrecy" Addy quipped.

Just then Hugh and Gene appeared and we joined them. Of course everyone was cordial, but there was uneasiness in the air. More than just a split. More because of the tragedy of it all. A dead baby. A ruined childhood. A family in crisis. And because of our work we were more than casual spectators. We are enveloped in it for a moment in time. The four of us decided to make our way to the area adjacent to juvenile court. Juvenile court was actually five separate courts. There was a court docket posted outside the court rooms. It looked like this first hearing was going to take place in court Room Four. Of the five court rooms, this appeared to be the largest. Not that it was a great big court room. It wasn't, however, it seemed to allow the most spectators or witnesses. I guess it could hold around fifty to seventy people in the gallery. Dr. O'Neil suggested that we all step into the ante room to sign in and let the court secretary know that we were here. We then went out into a large waiting area. There seemed to be a lot of people, but I wasn't sure if that was related to our case or just the volume from the other court rooms as well. Addy and I decided to freshen up in the ladies room before we ran out of time. I couldn't decide if my coffee had metabolized quickly or if my anxiety was to blame for the need to go. Probably both. When we came back to the large area the hour passed quickly and before I realized it Addy and I were greeted by a woman who appeared to be in her mid-thirties. She was tall, slender, and had kind eyes. She was dressed in a simple gray suit with a white blouse and introduced herself as Miriam Whitworth, a victim's advocate. She asked that we follow her and that she would explain further. Addy and I followed her into a hallway the seemed to wind around behind the court room that ended in a cluster of offices. Ms. Whitworth escorted us to a small office with a table where she offered us each a seat. She sat down with us and said that she had been asked by the prosecution attorneys to meet with us.

"How come?" I asked.

"Well. This is an unusual case. The prosecuting attorneys want to make sure that you feel at ease and are aware of circumstances that might be difficult for you both. First of all because this is a high profile case, there will be an unusual number of reporters here. You'll see the cameras set up outside the court house. But there are also a large number of reporters just 'hanging' out in hopes of getting a scoop or two. For this reason it will be important for you to have no discussions regarding the case outside the courtroom."

"That makes sense. I noticed quite a few good looking single men with three piece suits waiting for juvenile court. Wished I had figured it out before you told me" AJ commented.

"It's the ones not in three piece suits you have to be aware of."

"Ohhhhhhh."

"The other thing the attorneys asked me to share with you is that as we progress in the trial, you may contact me for anything. Any questions, really anything. That's my role."

I started to ask her why us since we aren't really victims in this case, when Melissa walked in and interrupted.

"Excuse me, you two. I need to meet with you and the boys now. You don't mind do you Miriam?"

Miriam smiled and said, "Of course not." As she left she slid her card to both Addy and I and said, "Don't hesitate."

Addy and I smiled as she left and Melissa quickly added, "You won't need her. I'll help you if you need it."

We followed Melissa into the Court Room where she

lined up Hugh, Gene, me, and Addy. Melissa huddled around us and began to offer "suggestions" for how approach the questions we might be asked. She made sure to say she wasn't coaching us, but just wanted to make it clear how hard this might be. She added, "Just support Hugh. He's the psychiatrist of record." I nodded and thought to myself how difficult that might be given the fact I thought we probably didn't view the case the same. But whatever. Fortunately Melissa Rubenstein's path and mine didn't cross often. She reminded me of a pit bull physically, and in her approach to life. She was stocky without being fat, had a wide face, dark short hair that had been highlighted, probably to soften her face. It didn't work. Today she had on a dark red very tailored suit, lipstick to match, and black pumps. She had a rock on her left finger, must have been three carets, with baguettes adorning each side. She also wore a matching, thick gold herringbone necklace and bracelet along with diamond stud earrings. Anyone even glancing at her knew that she was loaded. As I tried to look interested in each thing she was telling us I couldn't help but think that she must be one of those people that is always on the go, and even when she relaxes it's scheduled. It made me tired just to think about her life. She was a partner in the law firm Asher, Rubenstein, and Robbins, the counsel for most of the larger hospitals in the area; was often seen in the society pages of Sunday's paper, as well as in the front section when representing high profile cases. I wondered if she really took time to enjoy her husband or her two kids. I just couldn't imagine it. As I began to ponder that more fully the bailiff entered the court and told us all to rise. The honorable Justice Melvin Sewall was introduced. Melvin Sewall was in his fifties, gray haired but in good physical shape. He was known to be a tough but fair judge. It was no mistake that he was assigned to this case. There would likely be no complaints about his handling of the court room. Court Room Four is a sterile room with canned lighting that does nothing to warm the gray walls and sharp corners of the mahogany wood of the judge's bench. Each side also has a large, straight lined mahogany tables covered with many legal papers. The prosecutor's table has it's papers neatly lined up as if there are chapters to this story. The defense attorneys are a bit more lax, papers appear less organized but there seems to be a system. Melissa's positioning right behind the prosecution seems a bit staged. First up is Hugh, but before Hugh even makes it to the witness stand the defense requests that the witnesses be "sequestered". The judge quietly contemplates this request, and with a solemn look states: "In light of the potential outcome to this minor child, I believe that is warranted. Each party to this case is hereby ordered by the court NOT to discuss this case with any other witnesses. In addition to this order, I am going to issue a closed courtroom order." The bailiff requests that the audience be dismissed. Melissa escorts us out and tells us to just stay put for now. She explains that Hugh's testimony may take some time. She'll let us know if we'll be dismissed and can go back to work, or if we need to stay. I lean over to Addy and say, "So much for following Hugh's lead." While Melissa can't hear me she shoots me a glare and returns to the courtroom.

About twenty minutes later Melissa emerges from court and tells me and Addy that we can leave. She tells Gene to stay put. She admonishes us to keep our pagers on and be available whenever they call. She said that Miriam Whitworth would call us and let us know when we were up. She also made it clear that this would be the extent of our interaction with Miriam. Melissa thought that Hugh and Gene's testimony would take most of the next two to three days. I glanced at Addy. She looked disappointed; I knew she didn't want to be here all week. Carl and the kids were in North Carolina on the beach and she desperately wanted to be with them. As we walked out of court, Addy said, "Great, Carl's going to be thrilled with this news."

"I know. Sorry I got you into this. I really thought this was going to be a slam dunk."

"Somehow when we work together on anything, it's never a slam dunk."

We hugged and parted ways. I went back to the hospital. I was assaulted by questions from staff asking my how my testimony went. I explained that I hadn't even started, that Hugh and Gene were up and I was the lady in waiting.

Thursday, June 26th

I was trying to stay busy with paperwork in my office when the page finally came. It was Miriam. I was to appear at court a 1 p.m. I felt the butterflies in my stomach acting up. I continued shuffling papers until it was time for me to go.

Walking into the court I noticed that it was yet another gorgeous Colorado afternoon; big puffy clouds in the sky, low humidity, and temperatures in the low eighties. I had fallen in love with this state. As a transplant from the east coast, I wondered how many natives realized how lucky they were to have this kick butt beautiful weather. I was quickly sobered as I walked into the dismal gray courtroom. I saw Jason Carter sitting next to Alana Livingston and Michael Kilpatrick. Behind them in the gallery was Mrs. Carter. She was clad in a bright yellow print dress and sandals. Her outfit contrasted with the overall atmosphere. The mood was clearly somber. I was sworn in and my credentials reviewed to establish me as an expert in my area. When I stated that I was a pediatric nurse practitioner, Melissa looked perturbed. I couldn't remember if I had told her that before. I knew that she asked about my education when we first got the case. I told her about my degrees, but I don't think I ever told her about my credentials as a nurse practitioner. First up, the prosecution.

"Ms Kiley. May I call you Ms. Kiley?"

"Yes, that would be fine." I responded.

"You are the Director of the Child Psychiatry Unit at Mt Washington. Correct?" asked Neil Oberlin. Neil was the chief prosecutor for juvenile court. We knew each other from several cases that involved clients we both shared, but beyond that we were merely acquaintances. "You were one of a team that evaluated Jason Wayne Carter shortly after his arrest. Is that correct?"

"Yes."

"Can you describe how you did your portion of the evaluation?"

I went over the number of times I met with Jason individually, how I spoke with staff regarding their observations, and how I reviewed limited information available to us from Social Services. I also described how I briefly met Mrs. Carter and Jason's older brother.

"Can you diagnose patients within the scope of your job?"

"Yes, as a nurse practitioner I can formulate diagnoses as well as prescribe medication."

"Did you prescribe any medication for Jason Carter?"

"No, medication evaluation was not requested by the court."

"Did you formulate a diagnosis?"

"Yes, I did."

"And what would that diagnosis be?"

As I got ready to answer I noticed Melissa shaking her head back and forth as if to say, "Don't say it. Don't even open your mouth." When I looked at the defense attorneys as well as the prosecution, I only saw interested faces. I went on, "I thought Jason Carter suffered from PTSD, Post Traumatic Stress Disorder."

"And what made you think that?"

I went on discussing his hyper vigilance, reports of flash backs, etc."

The prosecution went on to ask about Jason's family life. I talked about his relationship with his mother, how he was very attached to her and often sought her approval when doing things. I looked up to see Ms. Carter scowling at me as I spoke. I had no idea why she would look at me that way. I wasn't saying anything bad about her, merely that she and her son were close. At the same time I once again noticed Melissa shaking her head.

The odd thing was the defense and the prosecution were simply interested, not overly so, just paying attention. The remainder of the prosecution's questions pertained to the formulation of the diagnosis as well a few more questions about Jason and his relationship with Mrs. Carter. Next up, the defense.

"No further questions, your honor."

Wow. I got off easy. Why would the Defense not cross examine me? Aside from Melissa's disapproving looks and Mrs. Carter's scowl, I thought it went well. I'd have to call AJ on my way home and let her know. Hopefully, her testimony would go as well and she could be off to the beach by Friday night.

CHAPTER TWENTY-ONE

Adrianna – Deceit

Feeling better after Susan's call, I decide to take a detour on my way home. My favorite local happy hour restaurant would be a welcome haven at this point. I can't go back to my empty household just yet. I picture Carl and the kids sunning themselves on the beach and think of the fresh, spicy shrimp cocktails that they must be consuming. Maybe I will order the calamari at s Tatro's tonight. I know the bartender and owners well, as Carl and I would frequent this establishment on a regular basis. They are always welcoming and will probably give me some well needed nurturing when I explain my current solo situation. Janine, the owner, has been to our home in Duck. She and her husband were celebrating their 15th wedding anniversary just as they came upon the one year anniversary for opening their restaurant. Carl and I decided that they deserved a week away and offered our home to them.

I make a call on the way to check on everyone.

"Hi Sweetie, how are you?" I try to sound relaxed and open to hearing about the day's adventures.

"Oh mom, you wouldn't believe what Jackson did!"

"Well Jacob, do I really want to know?" I love the way he giggles and it reminds me of how much I miss all of them.

"Well, Dad was reading and relaxing in the hot tub last night, it got a little cold when we were walking on the beach crab hunting, yeah, well anyway, Dad was in the hot tub and Jackson threw a big, giant crab in there. It was so funny mom! We all thought that Dad was going to have a heart attack. He is still pretty mad and Jackson was not allowed to swim all day today."

"Well, I hope that Daddy is still in one piece, was the crab hungry?"

"Oh mom, he was out of there so fast, Ok, let me finish, sorry mom, Jonah wants to talk. I miss you mom. Are you going to be able to come at all?"

"Honey, I am so sorry. I miss all of you too. I would like nothing more than to be right there with you, but I have not been called to talk at the court yet and still need to give the judge some information. I have to just wait my turn. I love you Jacob."

"Ok mom, love you and here's Jonah."

"Hi Mom. How is it going? Have you testified yet?"

"No Mr. J man I have not. I am running out of patience on this one. How is it going? Is Dad managing all right?"

"Sure, he is fine. We picked up some pool babes and everything has been awesome since then."

"Funny, Jonah. Really, how is everyone?"

"Well, Dad is trying really hard, but he seems a little stressed and preoccupied."

"I am sorry Jonah. I am sure that it has been a very big disappointment for everyone, especially since I am the one who suggested the family time away. I would change things if I could. I love you, can you put Dad on?" I am almost to Tatro's and I don't really want to continue this conversation much longer. I am feeling worse than before and know that I will ruminate on these conversations all night.

"Hi honey, I miss you. Sounds like the kids are having fun at your expense."

"Oh, you heard about Jackson's crab boil did you? Yah, very funny. How are you holding up?"

"Not so well, I have not testified yet. Good news is that Susan did today and said that it went really well so I should be up first thing in the morning."

"Are you nervous?"

"No, on the contrary, I am just mad that I am not with you. I am really sorry about this Carl."

"Hey, don't worry, we are having a good time and the beach babes are treating us well."

"Nice try, you and Jonah have to get your stories straight if you are going to try to make me jealous, he called them pool babes."

"I tell you, that boy gives it away every time. Should I call you in the morning to give you a pep talk?"

"That would be nice honey. I really do appreciate your support Carl. It has been a long week waiting and wondering. Being sequestered has me really nervous, knowing that I already feel this split."

"Don't over think this; women always over think things. Hey, Jackson is asleep in front of the tube; I will kiss him for you. Try to get some rest. I love you Addy."

"Love you honey."

Tatro's parking lot is full. Thursday night of course. Janine always has great music and drink specials on Thursday. I park on the outskirts of the parking lot, turn my phone to vibrate and sprint for the door. The atmosphere is always inviting. This little haven tucked away in the back of a strip mall is heaven right now. The curtain on the door makes the statement that this is a respectable establishment. The dim lighting and contemporary furniture offer an ambiance that immediately relaxes the soul. The bar stools are very comfortable, with puffy leather seats and supportive cherry wood backs. The lounge also offers soft, snuggle seating on multi colored, micro fiber couches and ottomans. The grand piano glistens in the light and beckons someone with talent to offer entertainment. The doors are open to the patio holding a number of tables and a lively crowd. Janine greets me with our usual hug and begins by asking where Carl is.

"You don't even want to get me started."

"What honey? Are you two ok? I mean, I don't mean to pry."

We have never shared any of our personal issues with Janine and Rick.

"No, no, it isn't that. Carl and the kids are at the beach house and I am stuck with a subpoena for the trial from hell."

"Well you have come to the right place to wind down. We have your favorite appetizer on special tonight and drinks for you are on the house."

"That isn't necessary Janine; you have to keep the doors open. Your company is plenty." As we head toward the bar, my favorite stool is occupied. Janine senses my disappointment and overall mood. She motions me to sit on the comfy couch and waltzes to the bar. She quickly returns with what seems to be a double Absolute Citron and soda with a splash of cranberry. Just the way I like it with a perfect orange slice as a garnish.

Janine frequently returns to the door. She greets her guests with a smile and a welcome that makes everyone feel like a regular. I am sure that this is what has contributed to the success of the restaurant. The restaurant adorns white linen table clothes and a staff that is very professional. The service is impeccable and the food a five star quality. Janine nods to the bartender who hands her a plate of calamari and a place setting for me. She delivers this luscious gift to me on a fancy tray. Yes, tonight this is a little slice of heaven.

The time was fuzzy, the bar emptying out, I realize that I am in no shape to drive home. I scroll my phone, trying to focus on any name that might bail me out. Not knowing how much time has passed, I find myself thanking Janine for the ride and promising to make this up to her. She makes sure that I make it in and the lights go on. Grouchow is licking my hand in an effort to get my attention.

"Ok buddy, out, out, I know. Just remind me to lock the door when you come in."

The sun is blinding, phone ringing and Grouchow is at my side. What time is it? Oh my God. I jump out of bed and try to orient myself. That was not a good idea. I don't know whether to vomit or to hold my head. I decide that I better get the phone. I stumble, stub my toe on the edge of the dresser and grab the cordless.

"Hello" I manage to mutter. Dial tone. Damn it! I head for the bathroom, wondering what may happen when I get there. Again the phone rings.

"Hello from the beach!"

"Oh" was all that I could get out.

"Honey? You ok? You don't sound so good."

"Hi Carl just overslept a bit, probably the stress of it all. Thanks for the call hon, but I gotta get a move on. Will call you later, kiss the kids." I barely finished my sentence, and had to sit for a moment. I am furious with myself. I should have known better than to drink on a night when my stress was beyond any reasonable limits. Court. Oh no. Where is my car? I don't remember driving home last night. Shit, how did I get home? Please have let it be Janine. I don't think that she would have let me go home with anyone else. Now what? A taxi will take forever, and to admit my drunken episode to anyone is humiliating. I will try to shower and see if my head clears.

"Hey sunshine, what's happenin?" It was the always cheery and sweet, Matthew. If anyone would understand he would. He has become a household regular after his divorce a year ago. It is all too convenient for Carl, Matthew and I to tie one on and only walk the few hundred feet between our houses. Neighbors and friends, we seem to just click. "I need a favor on this bright, well very bright, morning."

"Lose your car last night sister?"

"How the hell did you know?"

He chuckles to himself and finally responds "Just a good guess, I knew the family was out of town and figured you might have gone to the watering hole for some company."

"Ok, I am due in court in about one hour, my car is at Tatro's, I am damn hung and probably need a car sick bag for the drive."

"I will be right down with the old Matt hangover kit, don't you worry sunshine, we will fix you right up. Just one question, you sober enough to drive yet? Wouldn't want you to get a DUI on the way to fry someone else's ass with your testimony."

Matt arrives with a 16 oz. Gatorade, two Tylenol gel caps and four Tums. He smiles the warm smile that says "hey, you have been here before sister, suck it up and march on".

"Thanks Buddy" is all I can mutter.

"I realize that there is a big case that you are working on. Carl said something about it before they left for the beach. Got you pretty stressed?"

"That is the understatement of the year. I am finally up today. Hope to be done in time for some hair of the dog at happy hour. Want to join me? I will throw a few your way for the kind rescue attempt this morning."

"I don't know, possibly have a date tonight, but let me see. Give a ring when you get out of the slammer."

I buckle my seat belt and realize that my phone is still

on vibrate. Damn, three missed calls. No messages. I don't recognize the number. It is the same number all three times and one of the calls was last night, the other two this morning. I don't have it in me to call before court. I need to get my thoughts straight. Traffic is slow and I am almost grateful. I am afraid that driving any faster I may not be too stable behind the wheel. Just as I am exiting the highway, my phone rings. God that is loud.

"Hello, this is Adrianna."

The voice on the other end was quiet and very firm.

"Addy, this is not a secure line, because you are on a cell phone. I can not reveal much right now, but I a telling you this as a favor to you and your professional reputation."

I interrupt, "who is this?"

"Just listen. You are scheduled to testify today. I would advise you not to do that without retaining your own counsel."

"Who the hell is this and what kind of game are you playing? Look."

"Wait, please listen and heed my advice. You will be humiliated in court. Go in and ask the judge for a continuance for the purpose of you retaining counsel. They have to grant this to you and it buys you the weekend."

"I don't want the damn weekend. I want to wash my hands of this case and be with my family and get back to my life. You are telling me to go into court ask that I have my own representation? I have a hospital attorney that is covering me on this one."

"And there, Ms. Jennings, you are mistaken. The attorney is representing the hospital all right, but not you or anyone else who disagrees with 'the hospital'."

I realize that this voice is familiar. He is trying to warn me about something. How would he know all of this?

"How do you know all of this?"

"I am allowed, by virtue of my role in this case, to be in the court room at all times. Witnesses are sequestered, the press is barred and there is a strict gag order by the judge. I am risking my professional license to give you this information. Please understand this is a very delicate matter."

"I am beginning to understand. You have the defendant's best interest at heart?" I ask this hoping to affirm my suspicions that this is the Guardian Ad Litem.

"Yes ma'am I do. I want this child to get help, just as others do; some others."

"Thank you for your trouble. I will think through all that you have said on my way to court. This is very unnerving. Will you be there this morning?"

"Of course, and my thoughts will be with you when you bravely ask the judge for his understanding in this matter."

I hang up and begin to panic. Am I imagining things? I know this stuff happens when someone is going through withdrawal, but I imagine I still have enough alcohol on board that this is definitely not hallucinations. Ok, try to make sense of this. What the hell is going on? I know this GAL and he is a straight shooter. He would not be playing games. I think of Ellen. She has been increasingly strange and controlling. She sure did not want Susan and me talking to that victim advocate. She is obviously protecting Hugh's ass. But what happened between yesterday and this morning. Susan said that all went well.

There are reporters everywhere. I decide to fetch the advocate's card out of my purse. Maybe she can help me into the building without the chaos of the media hounding me. I don't think that I can handle anything stuck in my face or anyone breathing on me. "Miriam, this is Adrianna, I am here, but so is the rest of the world. Can you help me get in there with less harassment than looks like I am up against now?"

"Sure Ms. Jennings. There is a place where the fence opens up on the side of the building, just enough for a car to enter a secured area. You will see both marked and unmarked cars and there may be a guard on duty. I will radio him immediately and get clearance for you to park in the back. The guard will direct you and I will be waiting at the entrance in the back."

"You are a life saver Miriam, and oh, we better not tell Ellen that you gave me this fine privilege. See you in a moment."

By the time I reach the door, I have turned my air conditioning on full blast. I am still clammy and remember my Gatorade. I chug it like it is never going to be available again. Ahhh! That helped. Hydrate, remember to continue to hydrate. I feel like I have not even taken a shower and that my pours are secreting alcohol. I despise myself at this moment and am even more anxious now about making a fool of myself in court.

Miriam is waiting for me. She holds the door and gives me a kind look and quickly looks away.

"Thank you" I say as I enter the empty hallway. This is actually much more aesthetically pleasing at the moment than the grand entry in the front. I am cooling off and decline her offer for coffee. She escorts me to a room and quickly closes the door.

"Have you heard from anyone this morning?"

"I have but it is all very mysterious to me though. Can you shed some light on all of this?" Just then, another advocate enters the room. She is flushed and begins to apologize for her presence.

"Its okay, I did not put the 'In Use' sign on the door. We were just about to head out anyway. The room is yours."

Miriam glances at me as if asking me to go along with her story.

"Of course, we need to get moving. I was just catching my breath." Miriam gives me an apologetic look as we are heading out into the frenzy of reporters that seem to smell a story and its witnesses.

"The people of Colorado call Adrianna Jennings to the witness stand your honor." The words seem to be surreal. I am once again feeling very remorseful about my consumption last night. I need to appear credible and strong. I stand up, surprisingly confident. I ask the judge if I may address the court. The judge motions me to walk forward, but not to take the stand.

"What is the issue Ms. Jennings?"

"I would like to obtain my own counsel prior to testifying in this case your honor. I might add that I am acting as a consultant in the matter and feel more comfortable with my own personal representation." Silence hovers over the courtroom for what seems to be a few minutes. The judge is kind and gentle in his response to me.

"Of course Ms. Jennings, I think that this court can understand the liability issues when consulting in such a high profile case, and if representation by personal counsel would aid in your comfort, the court will recognize this as a valid reason to recess until Monday. You will however, be responsible to retain counsel at your expense and will have your counsel present for your testimony on Monday."

"Thank you, your honor. I appreciate your understanding in this matter and I will comply with your orders sir. I will appear in this court room prepared to testify on Monday with my own counsel present."

Court is adjourned for the day.

I have to wonder if the judge wanted to hit the Friday Happy Hour specials early, or if he was being genuine. I thought that I detected a glance from him that he was supportive of my actions today, but I could be completely mistaken. What the hell happened in that courtroom that changed the whole momentum of this trial? It is a chance, but I have to take it.

I am shaking as I dial, hoping that I am doing the right thing and that my instincts were real.

"Hello, Tom Barrows here."

"This is Addy. We need to talk. Can you meet me at my office?"

"Don't think that is a good idea. How about Wal-Mart on Parker Road?"

"You are kidding right?"

"No, we will be discreet, move quickly and blend in. I tell you this is very sensitive."

"I am close, 15 minutes? By the craft area, it is near the fabric department, to the right of the camera area."

"How about just in the card section? I can find that."

"Oh sure, see you there in 15."

Wal-Mart is full of people in a hurry and people with way too much time on their hands. I grab a small, hand held, shopping basket. I need to look like a real shopper. I scurry toward the card section which is visible from the entry way. I begin to read cards and think that I may actually have a few moments to shop for upcoming events, when I feel a light tap on my shoulder and look up to find Tom Barrows.

"We have very little time to discuss this. I need to be really clear with you that I respect you and I want what is best for my client and feel that it is therefore ethically necessary to have this conversation."

"Stop the bullshit. We are both ethical people, I know that there is something going on here that is not right, just tell me what the hell it is!"

"Ok, quick and to the point. You guys have an obvious difference of opinion; there is a split with the 'evaluative staff'. The hospital attorney fought hard for you and Susan to never testify. The defense team insisted upon it. So, when Susan testified, and did a very good job by the way, your trusty hospital attorney ripped her to shreds. As soon as Susan exited the courtroom, Ellen stood and hollered 'Objection your honor, this woman does not have the credentials to be testifying as an expert witness and her entire testimony should be struck from the record'."

"What?"

"Look Adrianna, it was so obvious to everyone, but we all felt a sense of powerlessness. I don't like the direction that this is going for my client and feel that a political agenda is the issue. I had to let you know before you walked in blind."

"This is great Sherlock, but what the hell am I left with? I have to testify and I have only a weekend. What can I do to make a difference?"

"Tell the truth Adrianna and do it with the passion and professionalism that you always do."

My next move is to call Jon Hollingsworth, the current Medical Director for Ward 1A. He is always level headed, that is why he didn't take this case in the first place. Please answer. Great, voice mail, damn it!

"Jon, it's me Addy. I really need your help and ASAP. Call me on my cell, and have your best defense attorneys name and number handy." I hang up and quickly call Susan. Another voice mail. I realize that it may not be wise to leave any message. I will try her later at home. That should be safe. I continue to drive toward the house and begin to compulsively check my rearview mirror. Oh come on, I tell myself, this is ridiculous. Who the hell would be following you? This is not about you. It is more bullshit hospital politics. As I pull into my drive, I realize that the daily paper is not there. Did Carl cancel the paper? Honestly, at this point I can't be bothered.

I decide to Nordic Trak and wait for Jon's call. Grouchow meets me at the door with a "so glad to see you" look.

"Hi big boy, want to go out for awhile. I am sorry Grouchow I am not up for a walk, but you can go out and chase bugs. Go on now, Go!"

I change my clothes and head for the basement workout room. Turning on the tunes I decide that the CD that I use for spinning will do. I crank up the tunes, turn CNN on silent and begin my trek. I am drenched and thirsty after 45 minutes of both intense exercise and a lack of any rational thought process. Exercise is the one thing that allows me to put my brain on hold.

Grouchow accompanies me to the master suite where I run a bath and turn on the jets. Shit, I hear my phone give a faint beep, alerting me that there has been a call. Damn it. How could I have forgotten the phone with so much at stake here? A message. That is good. I dial the number that Jon has left on my voice mail, realizing that I am intruding on this individual's privacy as his home phone rings on.

"Hello" a female voice answers.

"I am sorry to bother you, but I am calling for Clark Festav, this is Adrianna Jennings."

"Yes, he is expecting your call, isn't that Jon a doll? He called to check with Clark before giving out our number, just a moment." Silence for what seemed like forever, then dishes rattling in the background.

"Yes, this is Clark."

"Thank you for taking my call, I am Adrianna Jennings."

Monday morning came none too soon. I am anxious to get this over with. I am humbled as I think of the pain that Mr. Carter must be going through, wishing that he could be in the court room while I despise every step toward the crowded entry of this center for justice. Hmmm, isn't that a thought to keep in the forefront of my mind today? Justice. I decide not to try the back entrance, feeling that getting through the media frenzy may actually toughen me up for what I anticipated I was about to endure. I glance around, searching for my new attorney. He said that he was tall, thin with dusty blonde hair. He was going to be in a blue suit. Deep breath, no counsel in sight. Make your way to the door I tell myself, as microphones are thrust in my face.

"Tell us Ms. Jennings, is it true that you are fighting your own battle here in court today and that you have retained counsel?" How the hell do these assholes get this information? I want more than anything to make some wise ass comment. I decide against this and push forward. The doors are only 15 feet away.

I pass through the big black arches and nothing beeps. I think of McDonalds and wonder why they didn't make these machines more attractive. A glowing yellow might invoke intense hunger though. No! Tell me this is not my counsel. There is a tall, lanky, Gumby looking character wearing a powder blue suit and waving furiously at me. Oh my God. His smile reveals a set of very crooked and yellow teeth, most likely from smoking. He saunters towards me with his hand held out.

"Ms. Jennings I presume?"

"Yes, good morning" I stammer, still not believing my eyes. Jesus, there is dark blue stitching holding the material together. Don't even look at the shoes. Where in the hell did this guy get this hideous outfit?

"I think that we are adequately prepared for your testimony, have you thought of any further questions?

Feeling ok? Get some good rest did you?"

Is this guy going to ever shut up? Hope to God he does not piss off this judge. Oh man, did Jon have the right guy?

"Thank you Mr. Festav, I believe that you were very thorough last evening and yes I am well rested thank you."

"Great, then let's hit it. Just remember if you get into trouble, give me two consecutive drinks of water and I am all over it to bail you out."

"Right."

"All rise." The bailiff echoed through the court room. I feel small beads of sweat lining my forehead. I can only hope that I don't have sweat marks on my clothes today. "The court calls Ms. Adrianna Jennings your honor." I slowly rise and Clark gives me a little tap on the hand, a 'you go girl' gesture. I make my way nervously toward the stand, raise my hand and go through the whole swearing thing. I am glad to take my seat even if it is the 'hot one'. Justice I remember. Justice.

The Prosecution is up first. This is the one that I always dread. They are always so forceful and they dance around until they pin you. I feel like I should be wearing a wrestling singlet, or suit of armor. We go through the usual qualifying as an expert witness crap and once I am seen as credible they begin. Clark told me not to look at the hospital attorney, but my eyes wander. She is glaring at me. Ok, back to justice. The questioning was relatively mild, and much shorter than I would have imagined. If the prosecution only took 90 minutes, the defense should be a slam dunk. The judge calls for a quick ten minute recess, but directs me to the only break room for sequestered witnesses. I am unable to talk to anyone except my attorney. The judge directs me to "not even use your cell phone."

While taking my place again on the witness stand I see a quick wink from Tom Barrows. This is followed by a 'hang in there' look. I am confused, but feel supported. My attorney gives a professional nod and we begin again. The defense attorneys immediately move in closer. They are very serious and tag team off of each other. After the usual questions about interviewing the defendant etc., they launch into a detailed investigation of my findings from the Department of Human Services Records. There are immediate objections from the prosecutions and an "Overruled" from the judge.

"Continue Ms. Jennings, please tell the court of your findings when you reviewed the documents from Human Services." Oh shit. I see where this is going. One drink of water. Remember what Tom Barrows said. Just tell the truth. Justice I think, as I begin.

"Ms. Jennings, did you review the entire record from the Department of Human Services?"

"I have no way of knowing that for sure, but that is what I requested."

"How many pages was this document?"

"I believe there were 1,348 pages in all."

"And you are saying under oath that you reviewed them in their entirety?"

"Yes"

"How much of this document contained information on claims made against the mother of our client, Mrs. Carter."

"Objection your honor", yelled the head prosecuting attorney, "Mrs. Carter is not on trial here, it is Jason Wayne Carter that we are attempting to focus on."

"Over ruled, but please show the court some progression in this line of questioning, continue and rephrase the question."

"Ms. Jennings, were there allegations of abuse in the

150

Carter household?"

"Yes there were."

"Who was the alleged abuser?"

"Mrs. Carter."

"Were there other allegations of abuse made by other potential perpetrators?"

"Yes, Mr. Carter was also accused of abuse."

"Was it listed who accused each of these individuals of abusive acts?"

"Yes."

"Would you please tell the court who accused Mrs. Carter of abuse?"

"I am not sure that I can recall all who reported, but I know that there were several neighbors, teachers, clergy and medical personnel who made reports."

"And could you summarize these reports?"

Your honor, this is third party information. The witness can not testify to this."

"Over ruled, the witness most certainly can testify to what she read in government documents. You are advised Ms. Jennings, to only testify to what you are sure that can be verified in the DHS documents."

"I remember that several of the Carter children were very dirty with head lice and unusual bruises at school. The thing that I remember about Timothy was that he went to the nurse at school and stated that he had 'hurt the privates'. The nurse called in DHS and a full physical exam was done. The results showed symmetrical markings on his penis. The item used to make such marks was not recovered and there was only speculation on who may have done this to Timothy."

"Ms. Jennings, it has been a long day and I have only

a few more questions for you. Do you remember who reported Mr. Carter as the perpetrator of abuse?"

"Yes, Mrs. Carter."

"And whom else Ms. Jennings?"

"That is the only reporter listed on all of the accusations towards Mr. Carter."

The judge realized that this was heating up and that I was at the end of my energy level. He called a recess until 8 a.m. Tuesday. I wasn't finished yet.

"I am sorry to do this Ms. Jennings, but I am going to have to order that you continue your sequestration in a location provided by this court. The bailiff will assist you in whatever you need."

Carl and the kids were due in at 5:20 p.m. and I was planning a very special homecoming. One more blow to the old family unit.

My accommodations were comfortable. I was given full access to everything but the outside world. Room service was at my beck and call, there were plenty of books, my laptop (without internet options) and a 24 hour watch dog, or court appointed sequester helper. I was able to call Carl to give him a quick update on the fact that I was tucked away in a secret location and unable to talk to even the children. He actually seemed very sympathetic. I think he heard the tears in my voice, though I refused to cry in front of the guard on duty. The guard politely dialed the phone to my attorney and left the immediate area. Clark was reassuring and told me that I was doing a great job. Nothing to worry about as long as I told the truth, this was not about me. Yeah, so why does it feel like it is?

The nice thing about being in this situation is that I did not have to drive myself. I was escorted in the back and able to wait until the last minute to enter the court room. I took the stand, feeling somewhat refreshed and ready to go.

The defense attorneys actually smiled at me as if to say "almost done".

"Ms. Jennings, I have here a series of twenty five, 8 x 10 photographs of the Carter household. All of these were taken the night that Timothy was taken into custody. Look at them. Take your time."

I reluctantly took the stack of photos. The first one, was very glossy and of a dead cat, partially decayed. It looked as if this cat was lying on some laundry in a laundry basket. My stomach turned. I quickly flipped to the next picture, a pile of feces on a bare mattress. Go fast I told myself. I whipped through them, not focusing.

"I realize that this is horrible and unconscionable, but please Ms. Jennings, this is crucial." I take two drinks of my water. Rescue me my 70's Gumby! He shook his head as if to say "Just do it". Oh great, a real Nike commercial you are!

"Ok, it's just a bit hard to look at." The series of pictures continued to portray an extremely hazardous household. The final few were of the baby. The dead baby. There were close up shots of foot prints on this plump, naked, Caucasian body. The next picture was a chain dog collar lying next to the baby on the floor. The final photo was the baby's neck with marks verifying assault by the cold metal dog chain in picture 24.

CHAPTER TWENTY-TWO

Jason - Religion

They tell me that I am going to be havin visitors today. Someone other than Mama. Though I sure don't mind havin Mama, it seems that she is mad at me lately. I have not even been around her, why is it that when I am not even there, she can still blame me?

I am wonderin who else might want to visit me. Probably some of those groups of people that ask me so many questions. They all seem to ask the same things. They want to know about feelings. Don't they get it? It is way more important not to feel. We get somewhere by doing. My Mama keeps telling me that. She is really clear that we don't give way to our feelings and that we do what we have to, what God wants us to do. She keeps telling me that when God tells us to do something we don't question it, cuz that is like questioning God and that will make him mad.

I have not been feeling so good. Nobody here seems to give a care about me. I feel like they forget about me. It is all business here and they treat me like a grown up. I want my art stuff and the snacks that they gave me at that other place. Is mama really going to marry him? He gave her a ring and that is that? We don't think of anyone else here? What about my Dad? He has the right to marry her. He keeps givin her babies. Right? That is "God's purpose for her bein here."

"Hey kid, it's me Henry. You in that brain of yours? Hey KID! You got some people here who say they want a visit with you."

"Is it my mom?"

"No sorry kid, its people from the church."

"You meant The Hall?"

"That's right, you wanna see em?"

"Ok. That's good, maybe mama sent them."

"Hi Jason, how are things going?" This guy is familiar. Mr. Johnson. He is a nice old man, with white hair. He has a nice smile. It makes me feel good.

"I am ok Mr. Johnson."

"Would you like to do some studying son?"

"No Sir." I always hate studying they make you read "the books", questions and answers, questions and answers.

"I mean, it is just nice to talk right now sir."

"What would you like to talk about Jason?"

"I don't know sir. Have you seen my mama?"

"Yes, as a matter of fact I have. She and the man she is to marry were at Hall this morning. We were all so glad that he has decided to study with us."

"Are they gonna get married soon?"

"Well, Jason, as you know, that is a very long process. I don't know that your mother will be able to wait, but we pray for her everyday."

"I understand sir. Is it wrong for Mama's to love their sons?"

"Oh Jason, God wants all moms and dads to love their children just as Jesus loves children."

Sirens sound as if they are heading for a five alarm fire.

"Everyone out of here, I mean it! You all back away and all visitors must leave immediately! The sound of the warden's voice scared even the most veteran of prisoners.

"Fight. Fight. Fight".

"What is happenin Henry? Henry?"

"Stop grabbin me! Who are you? I think that I am going to fall down."

"Its ok kid, Henry sent me to make sure you get back safe. He is dealing with the other prisoners. Don't worry."

That was weird. I hate this place sometimes. I wonder what Mr. Johnson was saying. Is it ok for my Mama to love me?

CHAPTER TWENTY-THREE

Susan - Defenses

I got a call from AJ. She wanted to meet me at Starbucks to talk about the trial. I was surprised how stressed she sounded. We met at the Starbucks on Smokey Hill Road close to my home. It was one of my favorites because it has lovely overstuffed chairs inside and intimate tables and chairs outside, weather permitting. Mornings there are often filled with lines of sleepy teachers and students from Grandview High School going all the way outside of the establishment. Afternoons on the other hand were quiet and the place was often empty except for a lone employee to serve.

It was not too warm, so AJ and I decided to sit outside in the shade. Frapuccinos for us both.

"How was it?" I asked.

"Horrible."

"How come?"

"Did you know that Melissa tried to have your testimony thrown out?"

"Get out."

"Yes, and did you see those pictures?"

"No. I wasn't shown any pictures."

"That house was so filthy."

"I remember that from the newspapers. I'm pretty sure it's being condemned."

"I saw that too. Anyway, I guess Melissa's motion to suppress was denied. She is such a jerk."

"So AJ, how did you find all this out?"

Addy proceeded to tell me about her encounter with Tom Barrows, the GAL and the tension in the courtroom.

"You know, the only thing I noticed was Melissa shaking her head back and forth and Mrs. Carter scowling at me. I guess Melissa's looks made sense. I suppose she's just protecting Hugh. You know, it drives me crazy the way Melissa takes over when she's supposed to be protecting the 'hospital's' best interest, not Hugh's. Oh well. I'm just glad it's over. I'm so sick of this. I'm ready to take some time off and enjoy the summer."

"Me too. I'm going to try to enjoy Carl and the kids every day that I can. I realized how much I missed them while they were away in North Carolina for the week without me."

"I am glad that they are back Addy and that you are feeling better about things at home."

"Carl was actually pretty sympathetic once he got over the initial disappointment. So now that the testimony is over, what are you doing?"

"Oh business as usual."

"Isn't Jon leaving soon?"

"Next Friday is his last day. He's been weaning himself from the unit for the last month anyway."

"Are you doing okay with it?"

"Now there's the loaded question of the week. What part am I doing okay with? The fact that staff really adore him and now they'll have to rely on me? The fact that his leadership has been consistent and I've depended on him to be there? The fact that the interim medical director is the one psychiatrist I can't stand and has no pediatric experience to speak of? The fact that most of the staff can't stand the interim director either and I have to put on my game face and act like things are going well? Which part am I doing okay with? Not sure."

"Oh. Guess I'm opening Pandora's Box. I know the staff think you and Jon work together well as a team. I'm sure they're worried about the loss, too. But it's more than that, isn't it?"

"I'm just plain going to miss him. Jon has such a gentle way of leading and staff seem to feel so secure with him. I can't imagine how tough it's going to be when they find out the replacement. Hopefully Dr. Levine's appointment will be truly interim, but I have the distinct feeling that Levine is trying to build his empire. This will be the third unit he's added to his resume. I'm not sure how he thinks he can do an adequate job, but we'll see how it goes."

"Susan, I wasn't talking about Levine."

"I know. I'm not sure I know how to respond. Jon is an excellent physician. I trust his work implicitly. And frankly he's been a great support since Adam's death. Somehow we had a connection with Elaine's illness and my loss. We talk. There's just a connection there. I'm going to miss him. But as far as work is concerned, it's business as usual."

We finished our Frapuccinos and had a little more girl talk. We hugged and told each other that we were finished with this case. I think we both knew that it wasn't really over, but for now we could leave it alone. As I drove home I thought about Jon. I was going to miss him so much more than I could imagine. He had this wonderful way with each of the staff. He observed closely, listened intently, and said little. It was the little he said that meant so much. And for me, it was knowing that he cared.

CHAPTER TWENTY-FOUR

Adrianna – Family Dynamics

My gardens are lush and in full bloom. August always brings an abundance of pleasures. Summer hockey is finally over, our schlepping cut in half. The boys are playing with neighborhood friends and burning music to CD's. Kickball seems to have made a come back and our boys are the homerun club. Carl and I have been taking long walks after dinner and finding new and exciting things to share with each other. This feels like a time of renewal. We are actively working as a family to connect with one another and to set aside time for the family as a whole.

Carl has been exceptionally attentive to me. He has put down the remote and has had romantic dinners waiting for me at the end of long days. We have taken midnight soaks in the hot tub with champagne and candles. Carl seems more patient. He is traveling less, though this will be short lived. We have taken a couple of weekends to ourselves in the Beaver Creek home. These have been unforgettable. The passion that builds with each nurturing act towards one another seems to sustain itself until our next adventure. I am looking at Carl differently. More like a true life long partner. This takes away the small irritation that everyday life brings to all relationships. It builds a sense of intimacy that our life seemed to lack. If this is midlife stuff, what is anyone complaining about?

Jonah and I have become very close. Maybe it's the parallel experience of our individual relationships with others that has brought us to this all time bonding. Jonah is in love for the first time in his life. He and Ashley seem to connect as soul mates. He is elated and terrified at the same time. Jonah is also struggling with issues of intimacy. He wants to be emotionally very open, but has not had the best role models to learn about vulnerability. Carl and I have probably shown our children more about how to be competitive than how to love another unconditionally. The kids, especially Jonah, have seen us fight over trivial and ridiculous matters. They have watched while we have assassinated one another's character and reduced each other to tears.

Ashley is the first person that Jonah has really opened up to. He shares most details of his life with her and she truly listens. She has accepted his flaws and very diligently tutors him on how to talk "feelings". This I find interesting. I am the therapist here and she is the one to provide what feels like treatment. I try to put my ego aside and to enjoy the changes that this relationship brings about in my oldest son. Jonah is funny and very quick. He is generally very easy going, but has a serious and sensitive side to him. He is insightful and has come to me more than once with that look of 'you seem to need support', followed by a very simple and sincere hug with "I love you Mom". These are the times that I try to imprint a memory in my mind forever. I realize that we are on borrowed time with the kids and that before we know it we will be empty nesters.

The twins are far less cognitive than Jonah. They have the most intense connection. This is the epitome of a love-hate relationship. They seem to honestly be frightened at times by how close they really are. They are like an old married couple who can finish each others sentences. They are together 95% of the time and seem to resent this, but would not want to change it either. They pretend to despise one another most of the time, but left alone are absolutely the most whole team I have ever witnessed. They are each other's best cheerleaders and worst critics. They will take the fall for the other and the next day hang each other out to dry. I sometimes think that I get it, and really understand it on a therapeutic level, but quickly realize that this is wishful thinking. They will most certainly keep me on my toes.

One thing that Carl and I have been successful at is consistency. We seem to click most of the time with our parenting. In fact, this is the sure sign that we are in sync. When the kids start to split us, we know that it is time for an adult retreat. We were not always so wise. We used to guilt ourselves into believing that the kids would be truly traumatized if we were to leave them with another caretaker for even a weekend. We have found that the kids enjoy the break as much as we do. They have actually asked when the babysitters coming. We have phenomenal twin girls who baby sit for us a couple of times a year. They are now seniors at Duke University, and are usually on the go. They have been an incredible influence in Jonah's life and we firmly believe that this has contributed to his diligence in academics.

Carl and I have thought about how life would be with a girl. We both agree that I am better with boys, and that he would truly spoil a girl rotten. I grew up a real Tom boy, not appreciating anything feminine. Carl loves that about me, that I am tough and athletic and very strong, but would also like a touch of polish to my nails. He loves when I wear a provocative dress and do my hair. He likes mild makeup and a soft scented perfume. No, I would have no clue how to raise a girl, do hair, or cry over bugs. We are very fortunate to have three great kids. We have been done with that phase of our life for awhile now, but I must admit, my fantasies do include being mother of the bride. I guess I better pray that I get one of those awesome and all accepting daughters-in-law.

Grouchow is hot and very lethargic. He hates the heat and just seems to think that he needs to conserve every ounce of strength. We are hitting the end of summer and I think of ways to motivate him. It is too hot for a walk. I will do my run after the sun goes down, after all this is the burbs. Grouchow does have one favorite thing, a car ride in the convertible. He loves to sit up like a real person in the passenger seat and make passers by laugh. He likes to cruise down the main street in our little town and have all of the kids run after the car asking if they can pet him. If I am ambitious I will take his leash and some treats and head to the park. Children love the fact that he is so gentle and parents appear relieved when Grouchow actually responds to commands like "sit". He is another individual in the family and one that I feel offers the most protection.

I think of the day's agenda and decide that since the boys and Carl are out for a charity golf tournament for most of the day, I will engage in my favorite hobby of gardening. There should be some incredible sales now. Everyone wants to empty out to make room for Christmas decorations. It continues to boggle my mind that stores see this as a positive marketing ploy. By the time it is really time to buy holiday items or decorations, most of us are so saturated with the hype that we just live with what we already have. I will hit Home Depot, Lowe's and two little roadside greenhouses. I have had my heart set on creating a new perennial garden at the North West corner of our property. I would like to focus on scented plants that can also be used in my practice for more therapeutic benefit. Lavender is my favorite. I like to mix this in with smooth rocks that I heat up and cool to just the right temperature. Clients can then hold these in their hands and experience the relaxing properties of nature. This is especially helpful when working with a client who has an anxiety disorder. The simple act of relaxing part of the body and attempting to connect this to their feelings is very empowering.

I guess your walk will have to wait old boy. I am off to the land of the living and oxygen producing. I will make it up to you Grouchow. I decide to put one of my all time favorite CD's in. I am truly not a fan of Country music. Our neighbor and auto hangover rescuer, Jay, gave me the CD of Big and Rich for Christmas last year. I can't stop listening to it. There is something very heartfelt about their songs. They have a harmony like no other. I carefully insert the disk into the CD player and decide that number six is what I want to hear: Holy Water.

Somewhere there's a stolen halo

I used to watch her wear it well

Everything would shine wherever she would go

But lookin' at her now you'd never tell

Someone ran away with her answers

A memory she can't get out of her head

But I can only imagine what she's feeling when she's praying

Kneelin at the edge of her bed

And she says

Take me away and

Take me farther

Surround me now

And hold, hold, hold me

Like holy water,

Holy water

She wants someone to call her angel

Someone to put the light back in her eyes

She's lookin through the faces and unfamiliar places

She needs someone to hear her when she cries

And she says

Take me away and

Take me farther

Surround me now

And hold, hold, hold me

Like holy water...

She just needs a little help to wash away the pain\she feels

She wants to feel the healin hands of someone who understands

And she says take me away

And take me farther

Surround me now

And hold, hold, hold me

Like holy water.

She says take me away. . .

    I feel like this is a song of reconciliation. It feels as if someone has lived my life and knows that I am truly sorry for any slips of conscience that I am responsible for. I also feel that a deep need for understanding and empathy, as well as passion are duly noted and accounted for. They seem to be mutually accepted. How rare that is. This is a group of individuals that sing from the heart and soul and produce a message that most can relate to.

    I arrive at a very crowded garden center. I finally see the sign: "60% off this week only!" I have to wonder what next week's sign might say.

CHAPTER TWENTY-FIVE

Jason – Clay

"Hey kid, got a therapist here to see you. Come on out. I know this guy. He is really nice. Might help you to talk about stuff."

"Yeah right. All they do is ask too many questions. I've answered the same stuff over and over."

The guard leads me to a room. Not the visit room where I see Mama. This was a room down the hall from my cell. When the guard opened the door, a short guy was standing in there. He had real nice clothes on; fancy clothes.

"You must be rich."

"No, not really, hi. By the way, my name is Dr. James Targon. You can just call me James."

"Ok Mr. James, what are you here for?"

"I will be working with you to try to help you get through some of this. I heard that you were really artistic, so I brought some drawing supplies and some clay."

"Thanks, can we use them right now?"

"Sure, clay or drawing first?"

"Clay sounds cool. What am I supposed to make?"

"Anything you want to. That is what art is isn't it? It is all up to you. Would you like to talk about your family?"

"Great, here we go. I knew that you would start to ask about something like this. Why does everyone want to know about my family?"

"Well, to be totally honest with you, we are trying to figure out what has created so much pain in your life that you would behave the way that you did. I wonder if you have some secrets that you are not supposed to talk about."

"So what if I do? I ain't telling you. I am in enough trouble."

"Well, just so you know, anything you say to me is confidential. I can't really tell anybody and my hope is to get you out of some of this trouble."

"How do I know that you are telling the truth?"

"How about this? Lets just hang out and do art stuff. The clay that I brought is called Sculpy Clay. Whatever you make I can take home and cook it in my oven and it will be like a permanent statue."

"I don't get to keep it?"

"Oh, no, I will bring it back to you. It only takes 30 minutes to cook in my oven. I can bring it back next time."

I like this stuff. It is fun to work with. WOW, I could make anything with this. I think I will make a person. They should have long arms and a short body.

"Ok, you gonna make something?"

"Sure, we can both make something then tell each other about it. We have about 45 minutes to work together."

This is cool stuff. I don't even realize that I am telling Mr. James about my big brother Spencer. Well, guess that it is ok to talk about Spencer.

"That is a very interesting piece Jason; do you want to tell me about it?"

"I can. This is a lady. She has really big ears cuz she hears everything. She has a short body, but really long arms cuz she likes to touch things. Her head is small. She has eyes that change color and a mouth that goes in. She is carrying a book. She likes to read to people."

"Very nice work. You put a lot of thought into that. Does your person remind you of anyone that you know?"

"Nope, not really. Gonna show me yours?"

"Sure. I made a person also. I have my person curled up. This person is covering their eyes and trying to protect themselves. I am not sure what is scaring this person yet though."

"Oh that's cool. This was fun. When are you coming back Mr. James?"

"I can come to see you two times a week. I will be back in three days. I will leave some clay with the guard and he will give you some supervised time to work with it. They will keep it safe until I get back here to take it home and bake it."

"That's real nice of you. Hey, do really think that you can help me?"

"That is what I am here for Jason. I think I can help you."

CHAPTER TWENTY-SIX

Susan – Business as Usual

Jon had been gone for a few weeks. I was adjusting to Dr. Levine's rather abrupt style of leadership. I had been having a number of impromptu meetings with multiple staff trying to help them to adjust with the changes. Fortunately it is summer time and the census is a little less robust. Most professionals attribute the lower census to school not being in session resulting in less stress for kids and families. The staff was grateful for reprieve in acuity on the unit and so was I. It was giving us the much needed time to make the necessary adjustments to adapt to our new leader. I was working in my office when there was a knock at my door.

"Ms. Kiley"

"Hi George. Come on in. And would you please stop calling me Ms. Kiley. Makes me sound like I'm about 100. Besides, I'm going to start calling you Mr. Gonzales if you call me Ms. Kiley."

"Okay. Susan. Do you have a few minutes?"

"Absolutely. What can I do for you?"

"Well, I know it's been awhile, but do you remember when I put the hidden camera in the nurse's station?"

"Yes, that was quite a while ago. I assumed you moved it when we weren't having any additional problems with missing medications."

"Well, I was going to remove it about a few weeks ago. But I decided to leave it since I didn't really need it for anything else."

"I suppose that's okay, but since we haven't had any more meds missing do you want to remove it now?"

"Well, that's what I want to talk to you about. I think you're going to get a report from staff at shift change that some meds are missing."

"Really? What makes you say that?"

"Well, I just happened to be in my office this morning when something strange happened. Could you come to my office so I can show it to you?"

"Sure. It's one o'clock now. That should give us sufficient time to come up with a plan if what you're telling me is true. Let's go."

We walked to George's office, located in a remote part of the basement of the hospital. It's small and completely filled with video screens that project images from various locations in the hospital. George had the video he wanted to show me all cued up on a separate video. Before he started it, he warned me.

"Susan, I'm going to let you watch this. You are the first person I am showing this. If I'm misinterpreting what I'm seeing, please tell me and then let's forget we had this conversation."

"George, what is it? You seem so secretive. What's bothering you?"

"Just watch it okay?"

"Okay"

George had the video rewound and ready to view. He pushed the play button and I watched silently. As I looked I felt a sudden wave of nausea, perspiration all over accompanied by too much spit in my mouth. I really wanted to go throw up, but managed to settle myself before I spoke.

"I see why you wanted me to look at this. Okay. A plan. Well, I need to page Judith. She needs to see this, too. And I need to make sure I'm on the unit for the count at change of shift."

"Sounds like a good plan, Susan. I'm sorry this had to happen."

"I know. I just never, in about a zillion years, would have guessed Leanne had a problem. On the other hand I also couldn't imagine any of the staff taking meds either. I do appreciate you getting me. Let me page Judith."

Judith Sellers is the Vice President of Clinical Affairs at Mount Washington. She directly supervises Leanne and is in charge of day-to-day operations of the entire campus. Judith is in her mid-fifties, single, entirely dedicated to the Mount. While I don't interact with Judith frequently, I have always been impressed with her judgments and her way of managing people as well as projects. She is a tall lanky woman who has tinted her white hair blonde and is always impeccably attired in a suit, shoes, and glasses that all match.

"Judith."

"Hi Judith, its Susan. Sorry for bothering you, but are you busy?"

"Actually you paged me out of a finance meeting that was putting me to sleep. What's up?"

"Do you have a few minutes to come down to security? I need to show you something."

"Sure. Do you want me to grab Leanne? She'd be thrilled to get out of this meeting, too."

"Uh. No. I'd prefer you to come alone and not mention anything to Leanne for now."

"Okay. You know whatever this is; I will include her in any decisions."

"I know. I would just appreciate it if you could come down now, alone."

"I'm on my way."

It seemed like hours before Judith arrived, but when I

looked at the clock, it had only been about five minutes. As she entered, she looked perturbed.

"Thanks for coming Judith. Do you remember a number of months ago that the narcotic count was off several times on the unit?"

"Yes, Leanne told me about it. Said you had a staff meeting about it and you haven't had any additional incidents."

"Correct. Well, George set up one of those hidden cameras in the nurse's station to monitor the staff counting."

"Oh yes, I remember George telling me about his plan. That was sometime ago wasn't it George?"

"Yes, it was. I ended up leaving it there because the camera wasn't needed anywhere else. So today I was monitoring all the cameras and I noticed something unusual. We'd like you to take a look."

"Okay. Let's get on with it."

George started the tape for Judith. I felt sick again as I watched it a second time. I looked at Judith as she realized what was happening.

"Oh. I get it, damn it. Why the hell would she do that?" She sighed and took off her glasses and began cleaning them with a Kleenex.

"So. What's the plan?"

"Well. I thought you might want to talk to Leanne directly. I thought I would be on the unit at shift change to be around for the count."

"Okay. Don't say a word to staff. George, I want you to call the Denver police and have one of their investigators in my office by 3 p.m. Susan, you come to my office as soon as the count is done. And Susan, you're going to be there when I talk to Leanne. It's your unit."

"Okay. It's 2:00 now. I'll go up and work in my office and be generally available around shift change. I will report to you as soon as the count is complete. And thanks Judith. I'm sick about this, but I appreciate your willingness to sort this out."

"You both did the right thing. We'll figure it out and determine the right approach."

I walked quickly to my office and was able to have a few minutes to myself to re-group before going on the unit. I took a few deep breaths as I sat at my desk looking out the window. After working with Leanne all these years I had grown to respect her. And now this. When I first started working with Leanne I found her brusque ways tough. Some who worked with her left because of her. I assumed that her irritability came from her years of working in psych. Psych nursing requires intense energy and finesse. Leanne had worked in several psych facilities before landing the Program Director role here at the Mount. She is about 5'2" and stout. She wore her jet black, straight hair just below the ears angled to be shorter in the back. The severity the lines of her hair created matched her personality. I can't imagine why she would do such a thing. I know she's complained about her weight and not feeling as energetic with menopause changing her body, but to put an entire unit under suspicion. I can't even begin to fathom this. Many of the staff regard her highly. It's always been difficult because on occasion her interference made it hard to lead. How do I help the staff deal with this? And to think that Judith is calling the police. I would have figured that she would have just made her enter a diversion program. There are two sanctioned by the Board of Nursing in Colorado. The programs are not easy to finish, but once done the nurse can keep their license. My thoughts are all over the place. How am I going to do this? Just then there is a knock at my door.

"Come in. Doors open."

"Hi Susan. Mind if I come in?"

"Sure Amanda. What's up?"

"I know it's been a while, but the count is off again."

"Seriously? What's missing?"

"Ritalin again"

"Same milligram strength?"

"Yeah. Whoever it is likes 20 mg extended release."

"Thanks Amanda. I'll make sure it gets reported."

"Susan, you okay?"

"Just a little tired."

"Don't stress about this. We'll figure it out. Sooner or later somebody's going to make a mistake."

"Thanks. You're right."

Amanda was so right, but I couldn't tell her yet. Brady left and I sat for a few more minutes before leaving for Judith's office. Judith's secretary greeted me.

"Judith's expecting you, go right on in."

"Thanks."

I walked into her office and was greeted by Judith, Peter Marrotta, the hospital's CEO, and Detective Brugman, from the Denver Police Department.

"Thanks for coming so soon Susan. I'm assuming the count is off again."

"Yes Judith, it was reported to me that Ritalin 20 mg extended release is missing again."

"That makes four episodes of Ritalin missing and the dosage has always been the same, hasn't it Susan?"

"Yes, that's right."

"I'm sure you all are aware, but I'd like to point out that Ritalin is considered a Class II narcotic" Detective

Brugman adds.

"We're more than aware of the implications, that's why we are including you in this investigation" remarks Peter.

"Well from what I see on the video and the fact that it's corroborated by the nursing count, I'd say that plenty of evidence for an arrest."

"I would agree" stated Judith.

She pushed the button on the intercom and asked her secretary to have Leanne come to the office. As I sat there Peter, the detective, and Judith worked on the details of the arrest. I sat mute, wishing I could somehow disappear. This was all so surreal. My boss, the Program Director for pediatrics, was going to be arrested for stealing Ritalin from the narcotic box. Just then there was a knock at the door and Leanne entered.

"Well, hello. To what do I owe to meet with this group of distinguished colleagues? I'm sorry; I don't believe I've met you." Leanne went over and shook Detective Brugman's hand.

"Detective Brugman, ma'am."

"So is one of our little cherubs in trouble or are we getting a new troubled admission?" Leanne was turning on the charm.

Judith was clearly irritated. "Enough, Leanne. I've asked Peter, Susan, and Detective Brugman to join me. This is not about any of the children. It's about you. Would you like to tell me what's been going on with the narcotic count or shall I tell you?"

Leanne flushed. Her ordinarily pale skin was flushed with color and there were splotches of red on her neck. "I'm not sure what you're talking about Judith."

"Okay. Then I'll tell you. You reported to me several instances of Ritalin missing. Correct?"

"Yes. That happened sometime ago. There haven't been any further instances have there?" Leanne was looking at me.

"Don't answer that, Susan."

"Leanne, perhaps you were unaware or perhaps you just didn't think it would happen without you knowing about it, but do you recall the announcements made about capital purchases during the second quarter update to the Board?"

"Yes."

"Then perhaps you remember that we upgraded the Security System?" Judith remained calm, but was clearly in charge.

"Yes." Leanne murmured.

"Then you knew the possibility existed to use covert cameras in the clinical areas, correct?"

"Yes." Leanne's eyes began to tear.

"And Leanne, do you remember our conversation about what you thought should happen to the person taking the Ritalin should they get caught?"

"Yes." Her eyes were downcast and the tears were beginning to flow down her checks onto her brocaded black jacket.

"I am so sorry Judith. It's a long story."

"Save it."

"Detective Brugman, I believe you are in charge at this point. You may use my office as long as necessary. Dr. Marotta, Susan, I believe we are finished here. Let's let the detective do his work."

We left the office. I thanked her and Dr. Marotta and excused myself. It was a long drive home.

CHAPTER TWENTY-SEVEN

Adrianna – Notice to Appear

Labor Day weekend is always fun, but this year was incredible. It was just us. Our family with no other kids or relatives. We went to the Beaver Creek home. We swam, and cooked, and played Scrabble. We hiked, took naps, and watched our favorite movies. Just us, all together.

There was a small antique fair, with interesting items for both adults and children. Our favorite dealers were there. They sell wonderful jewelry and small items from England. They always had new castle keys for the kids. They see us coming and remind the kids that the keys are hidden and there is a special prize for the one who finds a key first. This was great as it gave us a chance to converse with our antique friends and to browse the jewelry. They always have new and amazingly unique pieces. Carl found the most beautiful bracelet that I have ever seen. It was individual white gold, squares donned with Baggett diamonds. They were placed strategically so that the design maximized the stones and each one became a dazzling reflection of light.

Returning to work would be difficult, as I vowed not to listen to any voice mails or return any calls. I also had clients back-to-back the rest of the week. I arrived at the office early, to get organized for the day and to listen to voice mail. I had told the answering service not to call me unless it was an absolute emergency. I also had a colleague who took non emergent calls for me. He would email a summary of calls on Tuesday morning. One more thing to review. I start my day with Starbucks Breakfast Blend. My coffee pot was clean and ready to go. I head to the phone with pen in hand and begin scrolling information on my message pad. Fifteen minutes later I am finished with this task. Not anything out of the ordinary. The coffee pot beeps to signal its readiness to offer a morning treat. My email is also fairly unremarkable. Mmmmm, I love the rich taste of java.

My first client is a middle aged man, small in stature. He is riddled with anxiety and depression. He has tried many different combinations of medication, to which he seemed to have intolerable side effects. He was now coming to see me two times per week and we are working very hard to help this man find ways to reframe his thoughts and to stop his rumination. Cognitive behavioral therapy is very effective in these cases. He is due here in ten minutes and is never late. We go for our full fifty minutes. During the middle of our session I hear a knock on my office door. This is very odd, as I have a sign on my door that says "In Session". Clients are welcome to wait in the waiting room, helping themselves to coffee and listening to soft music. The knock continues.

"Excuse me, I am sorry for the interruption." I see my client's face, he begins to look frightened.

"I am sure that this is nothing, I will be right back." I give him a reassuring look and step out into the waiting area.

"Ms. Adrianna Jennings?"

"Yes, that is me, I am with a client, what is it that you need?" Just then I notice the all too familiar envelope from the county.

"A subpoena ma'am, sorry to bother you, but there was a rush on this one."

I finish with my client and review the "Notice to Appear". This must be a mistake. It is asking for me to appear tomorrow regarding Jason Wayne Carter. I thought that this was over. What could this be about? Before I know it, my next client is here. I certainly don't feel like listening to anyone else. I am completely unnerved at this point. I inform my client that I need to make a quick call and will be with him shortly. I call my new attorney, the one in the powder blue suit, and I am sent immediately to voice mail. I leave a message that it is urgent that I speak with him and could he please call me around noon.

I continue with my day, trying to concentrate on the issues of others. I have three messages by 11:50 a.m. Thank God one is my attorney. Unfortunately he is out of town, but will leave his phone on. I immediately dial.

"Hey Adrianna, so nice to hear from you, I am all ears."

"I thought the Jason Wayne Carter thing was over. I got another subpoena today, for court tomorrow. What is going on?"

"Well, don't worry, this is not unusual in such a high profile case, they must just need some clarification on some issues, sometimes new evidence is admitted. I wouldn't worry. Just go and do what you did last time."

"Can you be there with me?"

"Sorry Adrianna, I am sailing off the Virgin Islands. How gorgeous it is here. You really should check it out if you have never been. But, back to you, my partner is in town and could go with you, though I really don't think this is necessary."

"Do you think that there is something bigger going on? It just seems strange to have such a lapse of time."

"Don't read into anything, do what you do so well and let me know how things turn out." I consider phoning Susan, but don't want to bother her or remind her of any of this. She would certainly call if she received a subpoena herself. I will walk this line alone.

My night was restless, I tossed and turned and my eyes are very red. I put on a comfortable, conservative charcoal suit. I choose a soft pink blouse to wear with it and some fused glass earrings. I put my briefcase in the car and am off to the courthouse. I pull into the parking lot. Just another day. There is no media and no big hype. I don't suppose that Miriam will be there to greet me. My attorney was off sailing in the deep blue sea and I am feeling really alone.

A brief interaction with the metal detector and I am headed to the coffee cart. I look up to see Tom Barrows, the GAL. He gives me a cautionary nod. I cordially say "Good morning Mr. Barrows."

"And back at you Ms. Jennings." We get our coffee and slowly make our way down the hall. He begins talking in hushed tones, starting by telling me not to look in his direction and not to show any reaction.

"Ms. Jennings, it is no mistake that you are back here today. The investigation has continued to reveal new evidence and your testimony is crucial. Quickly, are there any pieces of information that we may have not talked with you about during your last testimony?"

"Well, let me focus, you have caught me off guard. I guess I don't remember anyone asking me about my interviews with the bio dad and the oldest brother."

"Will this be helpful for the attorneys to question you about?"

"I guess it would be. Nobody seems interested in the family's history."

"On the contrary Ms. Jennings. Sorry I can not say any more. Remember your testimony is crucial."

The court room was quiet. I placed my briefcase on the bench next to me. I begin reviewing a legal brief on another case in an effort to distract myself. Who would be in here today? I take a quick look around. Both sets of attorneys have taken their positions. There are two security guards, which I find a bit odd. There are no other witnesses there at this time. There must still be an order for sequestration. The bailiff enters the door at the back of the room.

"All rise". As the judge enters the court room and climbs to his perch, there is a noise at the back of the room. I turn as I move to sit and see Mrs. Carter being escorted by some court personnel.

"The Prosecution calls Ms. Adrianna Jennings your honor."

"Ms. Jennings, please rise and proceed to the witness stand. Do you swear to tell the truth the whole truth and nothing but the truth?"

"I do your honor."

"Please sit then Ms. Jennings."

"Good morning Ms. Jennings, you may remember me, I am the lead attorney for the prosecution. I am sorry to have your schedule disrupted at such late notice. We have some information that we need clarified, and may have some further questions for you. Are you ready to begin?"

"Yes sir."

"Ok, first of all, you mentioned in your earlier testimony that Jason Wayne Carter would make use of art supplies that you got for him. Did you look at these drawings?"

"Yes I did."

"Did you have any impressions of these drawings by Jason Carter? And if so, would you please give the court a summary of your impressions."

"First of all, yes I did look at these drawings, I studied them intently at times. This was a child that was having a great deal of difficulty expressing himself verbally. He used his drawing to calm himself and to express himself. There was a lot of rage in his work. This was evidenced by the sharp lines and dark red and charcoal colors that he chose. He would draw eyes that were very detailed, and to me looked frightening."

"Did you ask Jason about his work?"

"Yes and he consistently refused to say much about it. He would vaguely say something related then drift off."

"Did you notice a pattern of behavior in Jason after he would work on his art?"

"Objection your honor," comes a voice from afar.

"Over ruled. Ms. Rubenstine, you have no authority to participate in this proceeding. This is no longer your witness nor are you in anyway representing her. Now sit down. You may answer the question Ms. Jennings."

I am dumb founded. When did she come in, and what the hell was the question?

"I am sorry, would you please repeat the question."

"Certainly. Did Jason seem to have any pattern of behavior after he would work on his artwork?"

"As a matter of fact, yes he did. He seemed to dissociate every time his work got intense."

"Ms. Jennings, is that a clinical term? Dissociate?"

"Yes sir."

"Could you please explain to the court what that means."

"Sure. This is when there is a problem with the integration between things like consciousness, memory, identity and the individual's perception of the environment."

"Let me clarify, for those of us who are not trained in Mental Health. Does this mean that there are times when individuals may not remember things about themselves, their environment and what has happened?"

"Yes sir that is correct. It is like their brains have taken a vacation."

"Ms. Jennings, is this a voluntary behavior?"

"No, in fact, in therapy we have to work very hard with individuals to understand their triggers and to actively work through the situation while remaining in the here and now."

"So, you said 'triggers', does this meant that we know what causes this, lapse in memory?"

"The general theory is that those who suffer from disassociative episodes have been subjected to long periods of coercive persuasion. This can be in the form of indoctrination or thought reform. Children are especially vulnerable to this as they have little to compare their environment to and have very few places to seek safety and support."

"Ms. Jennings, this brings me to the next aspect of my curiosity. Was it your job as the 'social worker, therapist' on the evaluative team, to look into the family history?"

"Yes, I do this in every case. My approach has always been based on family systems theory, meaning that each individual is a product of the interaction of the family as a whole. I believe in treating the family along with the individual and there is research to substantiate the increase in success rates with this approach."

"What kind of investigation did you to with this case?"

"Well, I reviewed the entire document from the Department of Human Services."

"I believe that we have covered this, I was wondering who you may have interviewed within the family?"

Oh no, here it is. I have a real ethical dilemma on my hands, I have to tell the truth, but what will the repercussions be for the oldest son and the father?

"Uh, yes sir, I interviewed both biological parents and the second oldest child."

"Okay, let's begin with Mrs. Melinda Carter. To the best of your ability would you please tell the court about your interview with Mrs. Carter?"

Damn, I hate this part, talking about someone in open court when they are sitting right there. Okay, drink of water and look at the attorney only.

"Sure, it has been awhile, but I had requested that Mrs. Carter meet with me on the unit where her son was being evaluated. We met in a small interview room. Mrs. Carter was somewhat disheveled looking and I remember a very strong smell of perfume. She was immediately frustrated and defensive, saying we were all 'nosey folks'. I remember trying desperately to make this woman feel more comfortable and to understand that I was trying to gather information with her son's best interest in mind. She was very distrustful and continued to try to control the interview. I recall her saying that Jason would get upset when Dad would come around and especially when he would touch mom."

"Excuse me Ms. Jennings, did she explain what she meant by touch?"

"I honestly don't remember, but I am hypersensitive to issues of domestic violence and I don't think that is what she was alluding to. She did immediately follow that with the fact that Jason understood that his role was to be the man of the household now. I tried to question her about this. She quickly became agitated and left the interview."

"Thank you Ms. Jennings, was there anything else that sticks out in your mind about this particular interview?"

"Yes, for some reason I found it odd that Mrs. Carter had on high heels with this particular dress. They were clearly not of the same style. The wrinkled dress was more like a conservative print, and the shoes were very high heeled. They were like a stiletto heel if I am recalling correctly, and the perfume, it was very strong."

"Now, let's talk about your interview with Jason's biological father. I understand that he is fairly hard to locate and is described frequently as 'homeless and crazy'. Is this correct in your opinion Ms. Jennings?"

"I did meet with Mr. Carter. He was incarcerated on charges of vagrancy. He smelled strongly of alcohol and was filthy, but he was very genuine in his discussions about his children. I asked him about interactions with his family. He was clear that he goes to the family home occasionally, but made it sound as if this is on the request of Mrs. Carter."

"Did Mr. Carter elaborate on this?"

"Well, yes, he said that Mrs. Carter would want have sexual relations with him and that this was religiously based."

"I am not sure that I understand."

"I am not sure that I do either."

"Anything else about this particular interview?"

"Yes, I had previously met with the second oldest child in the family, Spencer. I asked Mr. Carter about this. His response was curious. He said something about that being 'risky' referring to Spencer's visit with Jason on the unit. When I asked him to clarify, he said 'she would kill him'."

"Are you, or was Mr. Carter referring to Mrs. Melinda Carter, killing Spencer?"

"Yes, but he quickly retracted this and then got up and walked away from the interview room."

"Have you seen Mr. Carter since then?"

"No"

"Do you think that Mr. Carter is reliable as an informant?"

"I can say that his thinking was linear and I felt that he was intact with reality."

"Fine, let's proceed with your interview with Spencer Carter."

There is a stirring in the court room. I can't help but glance at Mrs. Carter who is glaring at me with evil eyes.

"Mrs. Jennings, please tell the court when and where you met with Spencer Carter."

"Spencer Carter was visiting Jason. Jason introduced me to him and then Spencer agreed to meet with me. Very reluctantly I might add."

"Would you please tell the court about your interview with Spencer Carter?"

"Spencer was extremely nervous. He articulated that he was very worried about his mother finding him on the unit. He began by telling us about his older brother, who was 18 months older."

"Ms. Jennings, you said 'we'. Who are you referring to?"

"Oh, I had asked a male staff member to accompany me during the interview, as I was concerned about the content as well as, Spencer's level of comfort."

"Thank you, please continue."

"Spencer talked about his older brother. Spencer said that his brother would say things and his parents would get upset with him. They put him in psych units a lot. He would be on a lot of meds and would be really out of it. Spencer admitted that their Dad used to hit them, the oldest more often. Spencer remembered that the more his brother told the truth to teachers etc., the more his parents would embellish his brother's symptoms. Finally his parents ended up sending Spencer's brother away to a group home and he never returned."

"Is there more Ms. Jennings?

"Yes, Spencer said that he stayed around to protect the others, and that he learned to be quiet. He said that his mama always treated Jason like he was special. He then said that his mama was really the abusive one. He clarified this by saying that his father was physically abusive and this was visible, but that his mother was emotionally abusive."

"Did Spencer give you any examples that you can recall?"

"Actually, yes, he said that his mother would come out of the bathroom with only a towel around her and that the towel would fall off of her when the children were walking by. She would then scream religious things towards the children, telling them how evil they were for looking at her."

"Did Spencer say whether or not he had ever sought help or reported this to anyone?"

"I did ask about this, he said that his mama would kill anyone who told anything."

CHAPTER TWENTY-EIGHT

Jason – I Love You

"Jason Wayne Carter."

The guard is calling my name.

"Ah, yes sir" I answer him fast so he won't get mad at me.

"Visitor. Follow me."

"Yes sir." I follow him to the visitor place and I sit down behind the glass.

I see Mama come in. Her hair is more red than usual and she looks upset.

"Hi Mama. Your hair looks real pretty."

"Thanks my little man. You are always so nice to your Mama."

"Mama. Are you upset about something?"

"You know me too well. Well darling, Mama is a little worried about what's going on with your case."

"What do you mean Mama?"

"Son, I can't talk about it here. You know they listen to everything. You know how close we are and I'm a little worried about that. You know what I mean?"

"I, I think so."

"Yes, my little man, you do know. I'm going to take a little trip, I'm going to take care of things. You don't need to worry about anything. I will come to see you when I get back."

"Okay Mama. I love you."

"I know you do my special son. And I love you too. Now go back to your bedroom and rest. Mama's going to take care of everything. Like I always do."

CHAPTER TWENTY-NINE

Susan - Testimony

Here I am again at the court. Why me? Why now? Haven't I been through enough? Okay, Susan quit feeling sorry for yourself and be a professional. I really need Addy's support, but I didn't call her, because she didn't want to be involved in this case in the first place. Walk in there, head held high, competent, and ready for whatever the prosecutor or the defense has to offer. The same court room, the same attorneys, the same judge. Poor Jason Carter, sitting in the orange jump suit provided by the State. There are different colors of suits for criminals. Orange means murder. It's an alert for the security guards to be extra careful. Yellow is burglary, theft, or other non-violent crimes. Green is domestic violence.

"The state calls Ms. Susan Kiley."

I'm jolted out of my self talk and realize it's time for me to testify. I go to the stand, take the oath, and review my credentials once again. Interestingly, I notice that Melissa Rubenstein is not there. Hmmm, no one to defend me? Well, no one to defend the hospital. Prosecution first.

"Ms. Kiley. I'm sorry to have to bring you back here, but I'd like to review your testimony."

Why? So it can be removed again. Guess I'm not supposed to know that. Smile sweetly and carry on.

"What were your interactions with Jason Wayne Carter, also known as Timothy Basil?"

Over the next hour and a half I completely repeated my testimony. All the same questions, all the same responses. Mrs. Carter is still glaring at me. What is that about? She is creeping me out this time. I'm guessing that this has to be done to get my testimony back into the records.

Thanks, Melissa. I really appreciate the opportunity to go over this all again. My heart rate isn't quite as high as the first time. My palms aren't quite as sweaty. Will I ever get used to this? Probably not. At least I hope I don't.

CHAPTER THIRTY

Adrianna – Duty to Warn

I love the fall. October always brings crisp cool air, beautiful colors and gorgeous harvest moons. My hours are filled with a variety of clients, the most common, being school phobia issues. I find that for the most part the parents are the ones with issues of individuation. I have been off of caffeine now for three weeks and I am finally starting to feel human again. I am not even doing the decaf thing, water and lots of it. I decided that it was time to get healthy again and to work on minimizing stress in my life.

My office is bright with sunlight and feels warm compared to the chill outside. I slowly unpack my briefcase to prepare for the day. The small red light on my phone is blinking, beckoning me to purge the voice mails from its memory. I am pleased that there are only six unheard messages. I seldom have time to return calls before noon. I generally spend my lunch hour trying to multitask. I begin to look over my schedule for the day and realize that my cell phone is vibrating. I don't recognize the number, this is always a dilemma. Oh, what the hell. It's either now or later. If I answer it now so there won't be any phone tag.

"Hello, this is Adrianna".

"Adrianna, this is Detective Gionatti. Sorry to bother you Ma'am, this is a routine 'duty to warn call'. Mrs. Basil made some strange and rather offhanded comments during an interview with her. We have issued a warrant for her arrest, but are unable to locate her at this time."

"Can you please tell me more detective? What did she say? And do you think that I am in imminent danger?"

"Sorry Ma'am can't disclose any more, just watch yourself now. Take care, gotta run."

I slowly feel for my chair. My legs are shaky and I feel lightheaded. What is this about? I try to process my thoughts and decide that maybe Tom Barrows would know something. I begin to search for his number in my palm pilot. Just then the phone vibrates again.

"Adrianna, its Tom Barrows."

"Oh my God, do you have telepathy? I was just searching for your number."

"Listen Addy, you need to watch your back and get out of town now, Mrs. Basil has gone over the edge. The authorities are searching for her, but no luck yet."

"I don't understand this. Why me?"

"We aren't sure, but right now you don't have the luxury of sitting around and psychoanalyzing this. Get going now."

Before I even hung up the phone, I found myself scrambling to pack up. This office is the worst place that I could be at the moment. I quickly dial Carl's cell phone. Damn! Voice mail. I page him 911 and lock up the office. I am headed down the stairs and run into my first client. Oh my God, my clients. I am out of breath and barely able to speak.

"Ginny, hi, sorry, I have an emergency and need to cancel. So sorry. Next time the session is on me." She gives me a very bewildered look.

"Adrianna are you ok? I mean obviously not if you have an emergency. Can I drive you somewhere?"

"No, no, but thank you and I really am very sorry. Gotta run Ginny. Same time next week. Call if you need anything in the mean time."

The phone vibrates again.

"Thank God Carl! I just got a call from a detective, I am being threatened by, you know the case, and well they are telling me that I need to get out of town. Then I got a call from the GAL and he told me the same."

"Addy, honey, slow down. Take a minute to get your self together. Where are you?"

"I am leaving the office. I thought that I would head for home."

"Fine, stay on the phone with me and I will meet you there. I am leaving now."

"Damn it Carl. This case has been a nightmare from the start. I need to call Susan and tell her, can you imagine what memories this is going to bring up for her?"

"Listen Addy. Let's do this. You come home, get some clothes and take Grouchow. Go to our place in Beaver. Why don't you pick up Susan and tell her that I will take all of the kids for a few nights until this blows over."

"Carl I can't let you do that. You don't need that stress."

"Look, I'll call Matt, he will help with the kids, we'll call all of our girl friends and the fun will begin. I will see you at home. Call Susan."

"You are the best honey! I could not ask for a better husband. I owe you."

"We will discuss what you can do in return! Bye."

I page Susan 911 and anxiously await her call. Traffic is moving and I am driving like a mad woman. I want to get out of town so I can begin to breathe easier. My blood pressure is probably over the top. Phone vibrates. I can't get to it fast enough.

"Susan, just listen. I need you to pack up your stuff right now. I will be there to pick you up within an hour. Carl is going to take care of the kids and Matt is going to help him. To make a long story short, I got a duty to warn call today that Mrs. Carter has flipped and has made some threatening remarks. Tom Barrows called me to warn me as well."

"I got the same call. What the hell is going on Addy?"

"I don't know, we will have plenty of time to talk when I pick you up. I am bringing Grouchow and we are going to my place in Beaver Creek. It is slow season and there won't be much open."

"All for the better. That sounds good. I need to make sure that my kids are ok. Carl needs to keep it light with them you know? Maybe say we are having a girl's weekend and it was a surprise. I am really worried that this will send them right back there."

"Ok, now remember, Carl and I were both there Susan. He will do everything to treat this with kid gloves. He knows what they have been through. Don't worry. I will have Jonah pick them up from school. You just call to ok that with the school."

"Ok, thanks Addy. I don't have anything other than my workout clothes and my sweats in the car."

"It's ok. I will throw in some things for you and I have cold weather gear up there. See you in an hour."

Home didn't have that same welcoming feeling that it usually does. I am now getting really angry and frustrated that this woman has entered my private sanctuary. My life, my safety. This is not fair. I realize that I have completely pulled the car in the garage and shut the door before I even exit the car. Safety first. At least I am going through the motions.

I am greeted by Grouchow.

"Hi boy, get ready for a road trip buddy. You have just become my new body guard. I have to pack and we are off. Go out now and bark if you see anyone." My bedroom is full of sunlight. I just want to be here with my family. I want to be with Carl and my kids. But I realize that I would just be putting them at risk. I throw some things in an overnight bag and head for the bathroom. Grouchow is signaling me that someone is here. My heart begins to race and I move to the phone. I am ready to dial 911 when I hear the garage door. Oh man, its only Carl. I have to get my shit together.

"Hi honey, it's me. Are you upstairs?"

"Yes Carl, I just had a heart attack, don't worry about me. I think a complete break down is next." By this time he had made his way to the bedroom. He gave me a very tender look and put his arms around me. The hug was filled with true love and understanding.

"Things will be fine. Don't worry. I won't let anything happen to you. I am going to make sure that Jake, the Sheriff in Beaver, does some regular runs by the house. Take Grouchow and your .38."

"Carl, you know how Susan feels about guns. She abhors them."

"Addy, she doesn't need to know. Take it if you have it you won't need it."

My tank is full, and Grouchow is already steaming the back windows. I am grateful that it is not rush hour. I head for the Mount and hope that Susan is getting packed up and is going to get out on time. We can stop at the market on the way and I have plenty of dry goods in the pantry at the house. We will grab some staples and maybe some good old fashioned comfort food. I decide that some music may ease my mind and find some James Taylor. Deep breathes.

Susan is waiting for me in the circle drive in front of the unit. She looks very nervous and even a bit disheveled. We are both going to need therapy after this. Oh, I think Susan is probably still in therapy.

"Hi, thanks for driving. Are you as freaked out as I

am?" I decided that this was as good of time as any to lie.

"No, I think that everyone is over reacting. Carl and I discussed this and feel like things will be fine." Well that is kind of true.

"You are trying to tell me that you are not scared?"

"No, we have Grouchow and who the hell would ever find us in Beaver Creek? They will find Mrs. Carter and we will return to normal soon enough. So, I say that we enjoy ourselves and play sleepover with just the girls."

"You are just a regular Polly Anna now aren't you? Ok, by the way, could we get some hair color and maybe you could help me. This whole damn thing is making the grey come out that much quicker."

The sun is moving west quickly. The days are shorter and the leaves are falling. The air is probably 20 degrees cooler at my mountain home. I pull in the narrow driveway and long to feel safe again. It does feel a bit better to be here and strangely enough it feels safer to be with Susan. That seems odd considering our past traumas together. I get the car in the garage and immediately let Grouchow out for a break. He is excited to be here and runs and chases some leaves that are blowing across the drive. We unpack and settle in. I take out a bottle of wine and two glasses and turn on the fireplace and stereo. Susan comes out of the guest suite looking refreshed and more at ease.

"You are right, let's make this fun. We never get away by ourselves and God knows that we deserve it!"

I call Carl to let him know that we are safe and to check on the kids. Susan is anxious to talk.

CHAPTER THIRTY-ONE

Jason - Questions

"Hey kid, somebody here to see you again. It's your GAL. The nice guy. He's got some stuff for you."

"Ok Henry. I am coming. What kind of stuff does he have?"

"More art stuff and some food. Real food kid."

"Hi Jason, remember me, Tom Barrows, your GAL?"

"Yeah, thanks for coming. Is that McDonalds for me?"

"It is, I hope that you like cheeseburgers. I got you big fries and a chocolate shake."

"You got some art stuff too. I've been here a really long time. Am I getting out soon?"

"Well, we are trying to help you get to a better place. By the way, did your new therapist come?"

"Oh, is that Mr. James? I like him. He brought clay and we both made stuff. He liked mine."

"Great, I thought that you would like him. How about your mom. Has she been to visit lately?"

"Yeah, she was acting weird last time."

"How so?"

"Well her hair was really, really red. She said she was taking care of things."

"Really, what things?"

"Don't know. She just kept saying that she would make everything all right. Is she helping to get me to a better place?"

"I hope so Jason."

CHAPTER THIRTY-TWO

Susan – Take Down

"Addy, I hate this. It's just too many memories. You did talk to Carl about..."

"Yes, Susan I did. Now stop it. Carl and Matt have the kids and you and I are safe. Now let's just stop this and relax. How about dinner? Do you want to eat out or in?"

"Let's order in."

"Good idea. What's your pleasure; pizza, Chinese, ribs? Oh never mind. Stupid me. Nothing's open this time of year. We'll have to make do here."

"Oh yeah. Duh. Between seasons. Glad we came prepared."

"Yes indeedy. Eggs, milk, we even have some fresh blueberries."

I cooked and Addy unloaded the car and freshened up the house. She and Carl had a gorgeous cabin secluded on three acres in Beaver Creek. They had spared no expense there was a fireplace in the great room and in each of the five bedrooms. There was a room for Addy and Carl, and one for each of their sons along with a lovely guest room. I have stayed here before. It is a sanctuary for Addy, a place where she and Carl come with the children to get away from the activity of their very busy lives. The home is decorated in warm earth tones, a Colorado mountain haven for sure. The guest room where I stay has a queen size bed and an amber overstuffed recliner for me to relax in later. I hope I can relax. I hate not being home with the kids, but I know it's safer for them not to be around me right now. Besides they adore Uncle Carl and can use the male role models for a day or two. I hope they find Mrs. Carter soon.

I finished preparing dinner and we ate in front of the fire place sipping our wine and eating our pancakes, an unusual combination. We were both pensive, not saying much during dinner, but as the wine took its effect we began to relax. Addy suggested we clean up and go for a walk. The sun would soon be setting and views are spectacular this time of year. Addy tried to rouse Grouchow as he lay in front of the fireplace snoring. This seemed like an impossible task until she waved a leftover pancake in front of his nose. That was all it took, he was ready. We put on gortex jackets that Addy had in the front closet, and headed out. It was brisk, probably 45 degrees outside. Many of the leaves were down and blew noisily against the mountain side. Grouchow lead the way and I realized how serene I actually felt. This time of year always makes me feel renewed; school has begun, the leaves are changing, and the cool air is full of anticipation of the holidays to come. Grouchow is sniffing around and seems delighted at the possibility of finding a squirrel or maybe a rabbit.

"Addy thanks for bringing me here. You must love this place for so many reasons."

"Yeah, Carl and I love it here, it's our safe haven."

"Okay. Mrs. Carter. What the hell is that all about?"

"Well. She must have cracked under pressure. But why were they questioning her and what the hell would she have said that made them so worried?"

"I know she kept looking at me during my testimony. I couldn't figure it out."

"Yeah, she looked really intense. I never gave it a second thought."

"What haven't we thought of?"

"Do you think her new boyfriend is in on this? Do you think he was so mad that it wasn't his baby?"

"No. No, I don't think that's it. I wonder if maybe

she became overwhelmed and frustrated with the new baby and took her anger out on the baby but blamed Jason thinking that he's a juvenile and will only serve a short sentence."

"I don't know. Something's odd about their relationship. She seems like she can't stand to be away from him. I think she would have framed somebody else, not him."

"Yeah. That makes sense. Okay."

We walked quietly for a few minutes, both of us deep in thought. Grouchow had made his way ahead of us toward the barn.

"Boy, Grouchow is sure energetic tonight. That pancake must have suited him well."

"He must smell the scent of the horses. We had them here all summer."

"Who knows who else lived at that house?"

"Yeah. It sounded so chaotic. Did Spencer say anything to you?"

"No, just that he was very afraid of his mom."

"Great, that's reassuring."

"Oh stop it. We just settled down."

"Yeah. I know." We walked to the barn, leaned against the split rail fence and gazed out at the spectacular sight. The sun was setting behind the mountains and I could hear the stream bubbling in the background. A loud pop jarred me from my serene moment.

"You're all wrong about your theories ladies." Addy and I both jumped and turned around to see Mrs. Carter pointing a gun at us both. I could feel my mouth go dry and hoped I didn't look as absolutely shocked as I was feeling. Addy spoke first.

"Uh, Mrs. Carter. What are you doing here?"

"As if you don't know."

"No, I'm not sure I do."

I could see the panic in Addy's eyes as she searched for Grouchow.

"You two smarties think you know all that, but you don't. Why didn't you just let those doctors do the talking? You could have just gone back to your stupid jobs. But now I have to take care of you. You two are just too close to be trusted."

Addy and I looked at each other and in a split second decided to take the therapeutic approach.

I said, "I'm really not sure what you are talking about, Mrs. Carter. I know you seemed upset at the trial. Honestly, I didn't know and still don't know what was bothering you."

"Shut up and get to walking." I felt the cold metal against my back.

"Where?"

"Back up to the house. That's a mighty nice house you got there Ms. Jennings."

"Thanks. How do you know that's my house?"

Addy was hedging. I knew that it was all that she could do to let thoughts of Grouchow be. It would only inflame and empower Mrs. Carter.

"Well, I suppose I'm smarter than you gave me credit for, now aren't I?"

"Yes. I'm sorry if you didn't think I thought you were an intelligent woman. You have raised your children almost all alone. You sure are a smart woman. But I still don't how you knew this was my house."

"Not that it's any of your business, but I have worked with the Hall to recruit new Witnesses. We were working on the computer and could look up anyone's name and then find the home and see it one of them satellite pictures. You have three homes, fancy aren't you?"

"I have been lucky. So, why here? What is making you so upset?"

"Quit talking and let's get in the house."

We walked back up the trail. Grouchow was alone and our body guard was gone. Mrs. Carter didn't seem too concerned about anything. We made it back to the front porch and Addy asked Mrs. Carter if it was okay for her to reach in her pocket to get the key. She seemed to like that Addy was so respectful. We went inside. Addy and I made eye contact again. Continue with the therapeutic approach. Thank goodness Addy and I had worked together so long. Addy asked Mrs. Carter if she could go get a drink. Mrs. Carter immediately said, "No. I want you to sit in those chairs right there."

"Please Mrs. Carter" Addy pleaded, "I won't even get a glass out of the cupboard. The air is so much drier up here. Would you like some water?"

"Fancy that, now she's waiting on me. Yes, I would like some water. Just one cup for me. You can drink out of the faucet."

I watched Addy as she went to the sink. Her kitchen has recessed lighting and gray granite countertops. Oh, I see. Her cell phone was charging on the countertop. As she turned the water on full blast, I tried to distract Mrs. Carter.

"Mrs. Carter, should I take my shoes off before I sit down?"

"Why, yes. That's a good idea. Get nice and comfy."

I purposely scooted the chair across the hard wood floor, hoping to drown the sound of the operator.

"911, what's you're emergency?"

At that moment, Addy loudly said, "Mrs. Carter, please put down your gun. It's only Susan and me here. We're not out to hurt you."

"Oh, you've already hurt me alright." Mrs. Carter didn't seem to have heard anything.

"Listen, bitch. Get over here. Bring me my water. Quit your stalling."

"Mrs. Carter, just what do you intend to do? Are you going to kill us?"

"Now aren't you the smart one? "

"Can we at least know why?"

"You're both fools, meddling into my business. Jason loves me. And I love him. And if you had kept your mouths shut no one would have figured out that this baby was his. He didn't know, still doesn't. But now the authorities have been running tests. Damn it. And it was something you all said that tipped them off."

Addy and I looked at each other, trying to stifle our shock.

"Quit looking at each other, in your coy little ways."

"Mrs. Carter, Are you saying that Rusty was a product of you and Jason?"

Addy was into her "court like" line of questioning.

"Are you dumb? Do I have to spell it out for you? Jason is the only boy that has ever loved me this much. I love him back the same way. He is not a little boy anymore. The baby, Rusty, was not supposed to happen. I thought that I was done being able to have any more babies. I am now being punished for my sins. That is why it doesn't matter now if I kill you."

"What happened to Rusty though? Was Jason so

jealous that he needed to get rid of Rusty?"

"No, my Jason knew that our love was different from all the rest. He was never jealous. No, me and Jason were pleasuring each other and that damn baby started to cry and fuss. I was getting upset. Jason hated it when I was upset. I told him to go quiet that wretched baby. The baby would not stop. He kept wailing and screaming. All I wanted was my Jason. I wanted the baby to go away. I told Jason to take care of him. Jason picked him up and was cuddling him. I got even madder then. I shouted at Jason. No you idiot, I mean shut him up. I threw the baby on the floor and he cried even louder. I screamed at Jason to shut him up. Stomp on him now. Jason was crying and begging me to stop."

Mrs. Carter was sobbing now. I knew I had to intervene. She was shaking. I almost wanted to comfort her, but realized this was our chance. I glanced at Addy and said "Takedown on two." Mrs. Carter didn't even hear me. Addy and I were like a well oiled machine. It's as if we were back at the Mount dealing with a volatile adolescent.

Addy rushed to her right side and I ducked at first and then made it to her left side. Addy was able to get the gun from her hand and toss it to the ground. We held her arms as we guided her to the ground. She was stunned and did not resist. We gently turned her over on her stomach and secured her arms behind her.

Addy looked at me and said "Do you have her?" Mrs. Carter had given up and was very subdued.

"Yes, are you going for the phone?" Addy was talking to the 911 operator as she moved towards us. She glanced at me and simply stated, "The police are on their way."

CHAPTER THIRTY-THREE

Adrianna – New Beginnings

I rolled over, feeling the chill of the morning air. I reached for the covers and sat up with a start. Carl was there. "Its okay honey, you are home. It's only me. I have some juice and a bagel for you."

I felt the tears coming. "Just hold me Carl. I hate having this happen all over again. I hate feeling so out of control with my emotions and having sleep be a nightmare rather than solace."

"I know babe, but you are strong and you are a survivor. The kids and I thought that it would be nice to take you to the beach. I have cleared it with their schools and we are leaving tomorrow bright and early. I have actually chartered a plane and we will fly out of Centennial. Just us.

"Talk to me about what happened. It might help."

"Sure that you are ready?"

"I think so. Start with Grouchow."

"The bullet entered his right shoulder and cracked the scapula as it exited. He lost a lot of blood and was unconscious. The police called on Dr. Allen, the famous equestrian veterinarian. He was able to stabilize Grouchow and operate."

"And?"

"And he won't be accompanying us to the beach, but he will be fine."

"How were the kids and Susan's kids? Did they suspect anything?"

"Hardly. You know Matt. He brought over silly string and turned them all lose in the back yard. By the time they were done, we had pizza and hot chocolate ready. They chose to watch Starsky and Hutch on pay per view. By that time, they were pretty much settled in."

"How about you?"

"Well, I have to confess. Matt and I were upstairs and an emergency alert ran across the bottom of the screen. It said *"BREAKING NEWS: TWO WOMEN THOUGHT TO BE HELD IN A HOSTAGE SITUATION - WHEREABOUTS UNKNOWN AT THIS TIME."*

"What? It was on TV?"

"Well I now understand that you were clever enough to dial 911 on your cell phone and said all the right things to alert the operator about your situation. They just could not figure out where the signal was coming from. The mountains were impeding the tracers."

"Wait a minute. They got all of that on tape? So is this going to be admissible in court?"

"I am sure that it is. But you will be happy to know that Mrs. Carter is now confessing and she is being charged with accessory to Murder One, child abuse, incest, felony menacing and attempted murder. There will be other charges and she will be gone for a long time."

"I guess that should make me feel safer. Somehow all I can feel is sick and disgusted. That child has been robbed of any normalcy. She made him kill that baby. She first molests him for years and makes him believe in some twisted way that it was all good. Then she impulsively directs him to kill. That poor kid. He will never be right."

"Tom Barrows called and wants you to give him a call when you feel up to it. He said that he has fairly good news about the kid. You can call him later."

Carl and I lay in bed for another 30 minutes just holding each other. I realized at that moment that our love was like no other. I was bonded to this man forever and him to me. We have grown together over the years and it has become a very natural interaction, even in the face of chaos. We have three lovely children and are moving in a forward direction with our lives. I am very lucky.

"Mom, Susan is on the phone for you. Are you awake?"

"Sure Jacob. Come on in here sweetie. I can use another snuggler."

"Good morning Addy. How are you on this gorgeous Colorado morning?"

"Okay, I thought that Jakey said that this was Susan. Who the hell is this chipper woman that I am talking to?"

"No honey, it is me. I am feeling a sense of control that I have not felt in a long, long time. I am taking some time off and staying home with the kids for a couple of weeks. We might even rent an RV and go where ever it may take us."

"Are you on something? You are supposed to be as traumatized as I am, even more so."

"On the contrary. We were awesome and we are the good guys. This time Addy it turned out the right way, and we had everything to do with that.

I decide that throwing myself into a normal routine will be the best. I announce that I am going to the supermarket and everyone should add their requests to the list. I need to go alone. Need some time to process. The market was bustling. I headed down the cereal isle and instantly became nauseated. What was this about? Oh God, coffee. The feeling passed as quickly as it had come on. A fleeting thought. No way. I start to do the math. My period was awhile ago, I'm guessing it's just all the stress. They said that I could never get pregnant without invitro fertilization which is how Jacob and Jackson were conceived. Should I waste the money on a test?

I quickly checked out and raced to the bathroom. I hate public restrooms. Sure enough there were two pink lines. I ran out to buy another brand, hoping that nobody would bother my bagged groceries. Once again, a + sign. I was shaking. Very mixed emotions. I was way too old to have a baby. Carl and I and the kids were happy. How would all of them feel about this? Ok. Go home and act normal. Let it sink in and talk to Carl later. Should I call Susan? No wait on that too.

"Hello, Tom Barrows here."

"Hi Tom, it's me, Addy. Carl said that you called and may have some information about the kid that will help me unwind this tangled mess."

"Addy, how are you doing?"

"I am actually ok. I realize that diligence pays off and that your encouragement was a huge part of my ability to follow through with all of this. Thank you Tom."

"Well thank you. The charges on Jason have been reduced. He is going to go to St. Christopher's Home. He will be there until he is eighteen and will learn to live life very differently. Mrs. Carter will never see him again if I can help it and she will be shipped to Pueblo, to maximum security. They will have to put her in isolation because those women would kill her."

"Wow, I guess that is that. I am taking some time off to go the beach with my family, but will probably be right back at it in a couple of weeks."

"AJ, I would be honored to work with you on any case. You are terrific."

"The feeling is mutual Tom. I know our paths will cross again. Take Care."

Carl was watching football when I returned from the store. He glanced up and immediately came to help with the groceries. I grabbed his hands and put them gently on my abdominal area. He looked at me strangely. I must have had a glimmer in my eye that told my story. He began to laugh and said anything to get through a crisis huh? Stress brings out the best in you Addy. There goes the college fund!"

When we talked later, Carl disclosed that he had suspected for a week or so. How could he suspect when I had no clue? This man knows me better than I know myself.

CHAPTER THIRTY-FOUR

Safety - Jason

"Come on kid. It's time to go."

"Go where?"

"You know. Your GAL told you last night."

"Oh. That place. What's it called?"

"It's called St. Christopher's Home."

"Is it like this, with the bars and all?"

"No, kid. It's like a big home with lots of kids and lots of adults. You'll go to school and live there all at the same time. You can do your art work there and you can play on the playground."

I think this guard Henry likes me. He kind of winks at me when he's telling me this.

"And kid?"

"Yeah."

"They'll help you with your problems and you'll learn to feel safe."

"Thanks, Henry"